"Don't kiss me. This isn't a good idea."

Did that protest sound weak?

He nipped at her jawline, traveled up to her ear and whispered, "Feels like a great idea." His hands curved over her backside, pulling her hips into his.

Graham's hands and mouth, his body for that matter, always seemed like the answer. He made her forget everything except for how her body seemed to zing to life. But she couldn't zing, not today.

Eve pressed her palms to his chest and eased back. "No. I won't be distracted by sex. I want your brother to back off with the media attacks and insults."

She turned, needing to put some space between them. Having him so close was difficult.

But just as she spun away, a wave of dizziness overcame her. The room literally tilted before her eyes. Her hand went to her stomach just as strong arms wrapped around her torso.

Secure against Graham's chest, Eve kept her eyes shut as she pulled in a shaky breath. The dizziness remained. This was her first symptom of pregnancy.

"Okay?" he whispered in her ear.

Not really.

* * *

His Secret Baby Bombshell is part of the Dynasties: The Newports series—Passion and chaos consume a Chicago real estate empire.

Dear Reader,

I'm thrilled to be part of this exciting continuity! With so many twists and turns, and a secret baby, I couldn't wait to start working on Eve and Graham's torrid romance.

A secret pregnancy is such a fun plot. I love to read it; I love to write it. But with two dynamic characters, this story was even more of a pleasure for me. Who doesn't love a hero and heroine clashing from the get-go? But there's a fine line between hate and passion. For these two, family differences are instantly put aside when their desires take over.

As a reader and writer, I cling to that independent heroine, the one who takes charge of her life and goes after what she wants. Eve is definitely that strong-willed woman. She's not a bit ashamed to have a secret affair with her family's most heated rival...not to mention a younger man. Business and personal lives certainly don't need to mix, right?

Wrong.

An unexpected pregnancy is one sure way to expose their affair. Now Eve and Graham must decide whether their relationship is worth risking stirring up the animosity in their families. Can a baby bridge the Grahams' and the Newports' differences? More importantly, will they decide to come together as one united family?

I hope you enjoy this latest installment of Dynasties: The Newports!

Happy reading,

Jules

JULES BENNETT

HIS SECRET BABY
BOMBSHELL

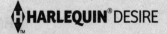

Special thanks and acknowledgment are given to Jules Bennett for her contribution to the Dynasties: The Newports miniseries.

ISBN-13: 978-0-373-73489-4

His Secret Baby Bombshell

Recycling programs for this product may not exist in your area.

Printed in U.S.A.

www.Harlequin.com

National bestselling author **Jules Bennett** has over thirty romance novels in print worldwide. She's written for Harlequin since 2008 and currently writes for two lines: Desire and Special Edition. When Jules isn't working on her latest romance novel, she's spending time with her family or procrastinating on social media. Check out all of her upcoming titles, appearances and more on her site at julesbennett.com.

Visit her Author Profile page at Harlequin.com, or julesbennett.com, for more titles.

This book goes to my shelf buddies
and awesome friends Sarah M. Anderson,
Andrea Laurence and Cat Schield.
Love you all!

One

Déjà vu swept over Eve Winchester. *Not again.*
This cannot *be happening again.*

The two pink lines mocked her denial.

Eve clutched the pregnancy test, gripping the side
of her white pedestal sink with her other hand.

Sheets rustled in the bedroom. Through the crack
in the bathroom door, Eve could see Graham Newport lying in her bed.

Now that she knew her predicament, she had
no idea what step to take next. For someone who
prided herself on plans, on spreadsheets and following through on details in a timely fashion, she
was completely lost.

But her unknowns stemmed from the fear of what

Graham would do. How would he react? How would their families, whose rivalry was legendary in Chicago, deal with this shocking news? The Newports and the Winchesters had enough drama on their hands lately. The Newport brothers' paternity had been thrown into question earlier this year. Graham and his brother Brooks were still up in the air after their paternity tests came back negative, but their other brother, Carson, had discovered who his real father was—Sutton Winchester, who happened to be Eve's, too.

Yeah, they were all in a state of upheaval right now and this unexpected pregnancy would just toss a stick of dynamite into the fire.

With shaky hands, Eve quickly put the test back in the box and shoved it beneath some trash in the can under the sink. Finally, risking another glance over her shoulder, she peered through the slight opening in the door and noted that Graham was still asleep. He had one toned leg thrown over white sheets, one arm stretched out to the side. Eve closed her eyes and pulled in a deep breath. After the paternity test had proven Graham wasn't related to her in any way, they'd finally given in to the feelings they'd fought so hard against. They'd been so careful to keep this heated affair a secret. But when their instant attraction had become evident, they'd both gotten backlash from their siblings. Fine, they could sneak around and leave the siblings out of it, right?

Yeah, that had worked for the past six weeks.

So much for keeping their families out of their private lives.

Now she was having a baby. A second pregnancy…this one much scarier than the last. This time she knew the ugly horrors that could happen. She'd lived through them, still bore the internal scars, and now she'd have to find a way to push through again. Could fate be that cruel?

Eve slid her hand over her silk chemise. Her flat stomach had once been round, once held another life taken all too soon. As much as she wanted to take her father's company global and focus on being in charge, she refused to let an innocent baby feel anything but loved and secure. And above all, this child would not be a victim in the war between the families.

That is, if she made it to full-term.

Fear coursed through her. The fear of telling Graham weighed heavily on her, but the fear of losing another child was absolutely crippling. Going through such grief again might very well destroy her. Added to that, her father was terminal. How much pain could one woman endure and still keep going?

The sheets rustled again and Eve knew she couldn't hide in the bathroom forever. Graham had come over late last night and they'd quickly tumbled into bed, as was their habit. No sweet-talking, no romantic walks for them. Eve had a passion for Graham and the family feud between the Winchesters and the Newports had no place in their affair.

Unfortunately, their worlds were about to collide in ways they never dreamed.

Stepping back into her bedroom, Eve pulled in a deep breath. Even though her entire world was completely turned upside down, she still had obligations, and Elite Industries needed their new president to be in top form at all times. The man in her bed would have to go because she had a meeting shortly and she needed to prepare. Plus, she needed some time alone to process her situation.

The second Eve crossed the room, Graham's intense aqua eyes were on her. That heavy-lidded gaze did amazing things to her body. Just one stare, one simple touch, and the man had her under his spell. The potency he projected was unlike anything she'd ever known.

With a cockeyed grin, he jerked back the sheet in a silent invitation for her to join him. He never had to say a word to get her right where he wanted her. There had been an unspoken agreement that this was sex only. Clearly they didn't want more because they were both married to their jobs and the intensity of their passion was off the charts. A committed relationship couldn't be this hot this fast. But they were about to enter a committed relationship of a totally different nature.

Eve shook her head. "As much as I'd love to take you up on your offer, I need to get some work done."

He raised one dark blond brow. "On Sunday morning? I can make you forget all about work."

Graham Newport could charm the crown from a queen…which was why he was one of Chicago's finest lawyers. Despite his young age of thirty-two, Graham had made full law partner at Mayer, Mayer and Newport. And it wasn't just the charm that catapulted him into his prestigious position. That reserved, quiet, yet lethal strength had him soaring to the top.

"Maybe so," she agreed, trying to sound casual, though the hidden pregnancy test mocked her. "But I have an online meeting later with a group from Australia because it will be their Monday morning."

Graham sat up, the sheet pooling around his bare, sculpted waist. Raking a hand through his disheveled hair, he sighed. "I hate when you want to be responsible."

Eve nearly cringed. If he thought she was responsible now, wait until he discovered the pregnancy. But that would have to wait. She needed to cope with this shock first, needed to make sure everything was all right. Granted, everything had appeared to be fine with her last pregnancy…then suddenly it wasn't.

Even though she and Graham had a physical relationship only, he had every right to know. But until she saw a doctor, she was keeping this news to herself. The last thing she'd ever want anyone to feel was the empty void and crushing ache of losing a child.

"You okay?"

Eve blinked, pulling herself back to the moment. Graham's aqua eyes held hers. Pasting on a smile, she nodded. "How could I not be after last night?"

Get it together, Eve.

Graham jerked the sheet aside and stalked across the room to gather his clothes. The man was completely comfortable with his body and she was completely comfortable enjoying the view.

Eve smoothed her silk robe with shaky hands before adjusting the covers and pillows on the bed. She needed to focus on something other than the sexy man in her bedroom, who never failed to satisfy her every desire, and the unborn child they'd made.

Graham would demand to know how this happened. She'd told him she was on birth control, and she was. But she'd switched types right about the time of the children's hospital charity ball…their first night together.

Strong arms circled her waist as she fell back against Graham's hard chest. Her body instantly responded to his touch and when his lips caressed the side of her neck, Eve couldn't stop her head from tilting, her lashes from closing and a moan from seeping out. She had no willpower when it came to Graham and the bedroom. Obviously.

"Maybe I could help you with preparing for this meeting," he muttered against her ear. "I do my best thinking in the shower."

Eve had been prepared for this meeting for weeks. That was her thing. She was always professional, always prompt, and she always had a plan B. Her spreadsheets had spreadsheets, and her period was never a day late.

Which is how she'd known when she needed to buy a pregnancy test.

And, if Graham really knew her, he would've caught her in the lie about needing to get ready for a meeting. He would've known she had her notes and speech down pat in order to win over the prospective new company. Which just went to prove, they didn't know each other very well at all outside the bedroom.

With a quick, effective tug, Graham pulled the knot free on her robe. Eve gripped his hands. "You may think in the shower, but I guarantee I won't be able to."

Graham playfully nipped at her earlobe and released her. "You're always flattering me."

As if his ego needed any more stroking.

Eve finished making the bed as Graham sat in the corner accent chair and slipped his dress shoes on. The man was hot as hell naked, but designer suits did some amazing things for him. And each time he showed up after work, she had a hard time resisting that *GQ* look with a touch of unkempt hair going on. How could one look like one needed a haircut and still have the entire Chicago power-lawyer look going?

It was the side eye. He had the sexiest side eye she'd ever seen. He'd tip his head in that George

Clooney kind of way and peer at you from beneath those thick lashes. Yeah, those aqua eyes were the main component of his charm to get you hooked. Once he had you under his spell, he pulled you in tighter, snaring you with the rest of all of his seductive ways.

"I actually have a case I'm working on." He came to his feet and rolled up the sleeves of his black dress shirt. "Brooks and I are meeting later. Say the word, though, and I'll gladly cancel."

Laughing, Eve shook her head. "We both have meetings. And if our families keep noticing how you and I are both MIA at the same time, they're going to stage an intervention."

Without a word, he closed the space between them, wrapped her in his arms and kissed her. Could something so potent, toe-curling and heart-clenching be summed up in such a simple word as *kiss*? Being kissed by Graham was an event, something she should prepare for, but there was no way she could ever prepare her body for the onslaught of passion and desire that slammed into her each time he touched her.

He ran his hands up and down her back, the silky material gliding against her skin. Nipping at her lips, he murmured, "I'll be back tonight."

With that whispered promise, he released her and walked away. Eve remained still, clutching her robe, staring at the neatly made bed and trying to figure out exactly how this unplanned pregnancy would weave into her perfectly planned life…and how Graham would take the news that he was going to be a father.

"Sutton will not win in the end," Brooks threatened. "If it's the last thing I do, I'll expose that man for the cheating bastard he is."

Pinching the bridge of his nose between his finger and thumb, Graham blew out a breath. Sutton Lazarus Winchester had always been a thorn in their side—his real estate business was Newport Corporation's main competition—but ever since they'd discovered Sutton had had an affair with their mother, Cynthia Newport, things had been much worse.

It had all started when she had first come to Chicago. Her real name was Amy Jo Turner, which she'd used until she fled her abusive father when she'd been pregnant with twins. With a brand-new name and town, Cynthia had gone to work in a coffee shop, saving money to raise two boys. She'd ultimately been taken under the wing of Gerty, a retired waitress. It was at this coffee shop that Cynthia met Sutton and wound up going to work for him. Cue illicit affair and their half brother, Carson.

The entire string of events was a complete mess. But now that the DNA test was official, Graham and Brooks knew for a fact Sutton wasn't their father. Which had made Graham's seduction of Eve possible. The woman kept him tied in knots. He counted down the time to when he could get his hands on her again, have her panting his name and wrapping that curvy body around his.

"Are you even listening?"

Graham dropped his hand to the arm of the leather club chair in his brother's office and sighed. He was half listening, half fantasizing new ways to make Eve lose control.

"I hear you," he confirmed. "And I agree. Carson is entitled to an inheritance when Sutton passes. It's only fair seeing as how Carson is his child, as well. The estate shouldn't just be split among the girls."

Sutton's three daughters were fighting this battle, as well. Nora, Grace and Eve weren't quite ready to welcome another sibling, but too bad, because the tests proved Carson was indeed a Winchester no matter how many people disliked the fact.

And Graham despised that he and his brothers were technically teaming up against Eve and her sisters. But it was only fair that when Sutton finally passed, Carson got his fair share of what was rightfully his. It would be in the Winchesters' best interest not to fight this matter because Graham would fight back…and win.

This entire mess was just another reason Graham and Eve had to keep their affair a secret and 100 percent physical. Nothing too heavy, no commitments and nothing long-term.

And no way in hell could their siblings ever come to know the full truth of just how hot their attraction burned. They'd not been too secretive about their initial attraction, but quickly discovered discretion was the best way to go. Considering what he and Eve did was no one's business, they'd opted to take things to the bedroom and ignore the turmoil surrounding them.

Keeping things simple—no talk of families or wills and Sutton's health—was the only way this affair was working and Graham was in no hurry to end it. A physical relationship with a woman who matched his passion like no other wasn't something he was ready to toss aside.

"So I need you to subpoena Eve."

The cold, harsh words jerked him from his thoughts. Graham sat up in his seat. "Excuse me?"

"I didn't think you were listening," Brooks growled. "We need her and her sisters to testify at the hearing regarding Sutton's estate. I need you to hand deliver those subpoenas."

So much for attempting to keep his relationship with Eve impersonal. Damn it. He wholeheartedly agreed that Carson was due his percentage, but he didn't want to go to battle with Eve. Not that he wouldn't win. Winning had never been an issue because when Graham Newport went into a courtroom, he was there for battle and came out on top. Always. But to get into a war with Eve... He blew out a breath. That would destroy this chemistry they'd discovered.

Not that he wanted anything long-term or serious with her, but he wasn't ready to put the brakes on this amazing secret affair they had going. And he had to admit, the whole sneaking-around thing did thrill him on a new level he never knew existed. Sex had always come easy for him, but to know Eve matched his passion, his fire, was something he'd never found before. So, for now, he'd really like to keep this subpoena out of his personal life.

"When's the court date?" Graham asked.

Brooks rested his forearms on his neat, mahogany desk. "Two weeks. I'd rather have it moved up because, with Sutton's health declining, I don't want to take any chances."

Sutton wasn't doing well at all. The man was on his last leg and Graham wasn't sorry the old bastard was fading. Sure, that sounded cold and harsh, but it was fitting for the man who was ruthless and conniving. The man had taken advantage of Graham's mother, whether she would've admitted it or not. He'd gotten her pregnant, unbeknownst to him, but he'd still tossed Cynthia aside when he was done with her. Clearly his high-society wife was all he needed at the end of the day, though she'd ultimately ended up leaving him.

Graham's own mother had recently died, too, which is how the paternity issues had come to light in the first place. But the loss was still too fresh, too heart wrenching, so he turned his focus back to Brooks. Letting the void in his heart consume him would be all too easy.

"What did Roman find out?"

The private investigator Brooks had hired to uncover Brooks and Graham's paternity had been working diligently on the case, yet hadn't come up with a name yet. They'd never known who their father was and, for a brief time, they feared Sutton was the one. Now that Roman Slater had found out that Sutton had fathered Carson and abandoned their mother, Brooks and Graham were out for blood. The only way to take Sutton down was to hit him where he'd feel it the most. Considering the man didn't have a heart, Brooks and Graham were going after his finances on Carson's behalf, and ultimately that would trickle down to his daughters. Graham ignored the guilt gnawing away at his chest. Business and sex were two areas where he never got emotionally attached.

"I'm waiting to find out, but he's almost positive he's uncovered more children Sutton fathered from his affairs. If that's the case, I won't hesitate to use it against him."

Graham muttered a curse and stared out the floor-to-ceiling window behind Brooks. The Chicago skyline was one he never took for granted. He loved his city, loved working here and taking charge. The ambiance of such a powerful city gave him ammunition each day to fight his battles.

"If he uncovers too many, they'll all want a share of Sutton's assets."

Graham crossed his ankle over his knee and raked a hand over the back of his neck. Maybe he should get a haircut. No. He liked Eve's fingers running through his hair. He liked the way she toyed with the strands on his neck when…

Damn it. He was here for Brooks. How could he concentrate when Eve kept creeping to the forefront of his mind?

"I thought of that, too," Brooks agreed. "Which is another reason I want this finalized before Sutton passes. So those subpoenas need to be delivered as soon as you can draw them up."

Graham nodded. He might not want to do this, he might hate mixing this business with his personal life, but there was no other way. And Graham knew Brooks wasn't usually this ruthless. But his twin was angry, hurt. They both were. With Sutton so hush-hush about what he knew, and right on the tail of their mother's passing, there was just so much emotion and nowhere to put it all.

Sutton was a man who deserved to be destroyed, and if Eve and her sisters got in the Newports' way, well…they better just cooperate because Graham would win this fight for Carson. Taking prisoners along the way wasn't ideal, but he'd do so for the sake of his brothers. Family was everything, after all.

Two

Two days had passed since the test. Two hours had passed since her doctor had done an exam and confirmed the pregnancy, assuring her everything looked fine. She'd held it together until she made it back to her car. In the quiet of the parking garage, she'd wept for the innocent life growing inside her and prayed she'd have the strength to make it through.

Just because children weren't something she'd set her sights on for her future didn't mean she didn't want this baby. Years ago she'd been naive and unprepared for what life threw her way. Now Eve was ready to do anything and everything to keep her baby safe and secure. She'd started taking vitamins the day she took the home test. At this point all she could do was relax and attempt some sort of stress-free life…as much as was possible when she was planning global domination.

As president of Elite Industries, she was more than ready to broaden the scope of the company's dealings. Her father had created a good foundation, but she wanted more. She wanted to prove to herself, and to her ailing father, that she could make this company even better. Before he passed, she wanted him to be proud of what she'd done.

Back at the office, Eve closed her eyes and tipped her head back against her leather office chair. Her father's days were numbered, there was no denying the truth that faced them. Sliding a hand over her stomach, Eve wondered at what point she should tell him about this next generation. Would he be excited she was carrying on the name? But if she told him about the baby, she'd have to tell him about the baby's father. Eve wasn't ready to expose her child to this ugly war just yet.

Once she told Graham, then they could decide when to tell everyone else. He needed to know; she just had no idea how to go about telling him. Would he be angry? Would he blame her or would he embrace fatherhood? How on earth would they deal with shared parenting?

Questions whirled around inside her head as her office door burst open and slammed against the wall. Eve jerked upright, shocked to see Graham striding through, her assistant, Rebecca, right on his heels.

"I'm sorry, Ms. Winchester," Rebecca stated nervously. "I tried to stop him."

What was he doing here? Nobody knew about their affair and they'd purposely gone out of their way to avoid being seen together in public. His barging into her office could jeopardize everything.

"It's fine." Eve shot her assistant a smile and nodded in a silent dismissal. Once the door was closed, she glared at Graham. "What the hell are you thinking coming here? The last thing we need is gossip about your being in my office."

Graham crossed to her desk and slammed a piece of paper down, the force sending other paperwork fluttering to the floor. "We need you to testify."

Shocked, Eve came to her feet and braced her palms on the top of her desk, completely ignoring the paper. "What?"

"This is a subpoena regarding your father's assets and Carson's interest in them."

Rage bubbled within her. This is why he'd come? Was this also the same reason he looked so angry? What was he thinking doing this to her, to her family?

"How dare you order me to testify against my father?"

The muscle in Graham's jaw tightened, a tic she'd noticed when he was angry with himself. So, that was the real issue here. Why was he doing this if he didn't want to?

What was going on and why was he doing this to her?

"You have to see what your father is, Eve." Graham's bright eyes held hers. Those same eyes that had devoured her body just yesterday now held so much anger, resentment. "Carson is entitled to his share of the inheritance. Plus, our PI has uncovered some other nasty facts regarding Sutton."

As much as Eve wanted to close her eyes to battle the pain, she couldn't. Her father may not be a popular man, but he was still her father and she wouldn't let anyone stand in her office and throw ugly rumors around. Yes, he'd admitted to affairs while married to her mother, but that was in the past. Couldn't people change? Did he have to pay for his sins forever? He was dying. Couldn't everyone just let him live out his last days in peace?

Enough. She refused to allow this to happen, let alone in her own office…her father's old office. Reaching for her phone, Eve started to dial her assistant. Instantly Graham's fingers encircled her wrist.

"What are you doing?"

She glared at him. "Having security escort you out."

The pressure around her wrist increased, but not to the point of hurting. "Hang up, Eve. Hear me out for two minutes and I'll go."

Still gripping the phone, Eve stared into his eyes, and her first thought was whether their child would have those mesmerizing baby blues. How could she resist him and tell him no when she couldn't get her own hormones in check?

And, how could she fault his loyalty for standing up for his brother? Wasn't she standing up for her father? They both held family bonds high and she had to admire that, but she still couldn't allow him to shove his weight around. Not here on her turf.

She hung the phone up and pulled away from his touch. Crossing her arms over her chest, Eve tipped her chin. "Two minutes."

A hint of a smile danced around those kissable lips. No. She couldn't think of him in those terms right now. The way he came barging into her office, forcing this subpoena on her had nothing to do with what they did in the bedroom. Right this minute, they were enemies…and soon to be parents. Talk about a conflict of interest.

"Carson is your half brother, too," Graham began in that steady, low tone of his that no doubt always had the judge and jury hanging on his every word. "He deserves part of your father's assets."

"Considering my father is very much alive, that's not my call," she argued. Eve hated discussing the fact that her father's health was failing, but the harsh truth was always at the forefront of her mind. "Is that all you barged in here for?"

"Eve, you have to see this is the right thing to do for Carson. Don't let Sutton's hatred and hard-headed notions trickle down to you. You're too good for that."

For a split second, Eve wanted to melt at his words, but then she recalled who she was dealing with. Chicago's youngest, fastest-rising attorney who marched through court and came out with a victory every time. He had Charm with a capital C. He oozed it and exploited it in order to get what he wanted.

"I have no hatred toward Carson," she stated firmly. Carson was just as much an innocent as she and her sisters were. "I simply don't feel it's my decision to say what happens to my father's things. He has a will, Graham."

"One that was implemented before he knew of Carson's existence." Graham pressed his palms on her desk and leaned forward. "Regardless of what you want to do, you've been served, Eve."

Part of her wanted to applaud him for holding his ground and having his brother's back. The other part of her wanted to slap him, tear this subpoena to shreds and toss it like confetti in his face. But she refused to let her emotions show.

"I believe your two minutes are up."

His eyes held hers for a moment longer, but he finally turned and walked out, his exit much less dramatic than his entrance. Once the doorway was clear, Eve's legs gave out and she sank back to her chair. With shaky hands, she unfolded the document and stared at the date she was due in court. Whatever was going on with the Newport brothers, she sincerely wished they'd leave her out of it. Her father was dying, she was pushing to acquire another real estate company in Australia and now she was expecting the baby of a man who should be her enemy.

What more could life throw at her?

"Ms. Winchester?"

Eve glanced up to see Rebecca standing in the doorway. "Do you want me to have security make sure Mr. Newport is out of the building?"

"No, Rebecca. That won't be necessary. Mr. Newport's business is done here. He won't return."

There. Hopefully that would help quash any rumors about Graham's unexpected visit. Rebecca wasn't one to gossip, though. Eve wouldn't have her as an assistant if she were, but she still wanted the utmost respect from her staff.

"We had a mutual client and he was dropping off some paperwork," Eve added. "Thank you."

With a slight nod, Rebecca stepped back out and closed the door.

So much for telling Graham about the baby soon. Now she had to figure out where they stood because he'd drawn a battle line the moment he'd opted to show up at her office. He could've had anyone on his staff deliver that subpoena.

Again, this proved how his family loyalties and his career were his top priorities. Which only made Eve wonder: Once he knew they'd created a baby, would she and the child be included in that inner circle?

* * *

The following morning, Eve's patience had run out. Graham hadn't contacted her since he'd burst into her office yesterday, and now the glaring headline mocked her from the front page of the paper: Chicago Kingpin Sutton Winchester's Infidelity Produces More Heirs.

She began reading the article and literally had to take a seat on a stool at her kitchen island when she hit the line about his "fathering numerous children out of secret affairs." Her stomach churned, and the nausea had nothing to do with the baby.

Tears pricked her eyes as anger rushed through her. There was only one family who wanted to stir the proverbial pot and that was the Newports. Brooks may be the ringleader in this agenda to bring down her father, but Carson and Graham were right there with him. And no doubt Graham had known all about this little media exposé when he was in her office yesterday.

Betrayal was a sickening feeling. But how could she feel betrayed? He'd never pretended to be on her side when it came to their families. They had sex, plenty of sex, but that didn't make them a couple. That didn't mean he had to be loyal to her or defend her to his family.

Eve knew very well who Graham was when she'd gotten together with him, so if blame was to be placed, she needed to point the finger at herself. She just wished she weren't getting so personally wrapped up in a man who was 100 percent wrong for her.

And what the hell was this about her father having "numerous" other children? Carson was the only child she knew of. Perhaps now that his secret son had come to light, others wanted a share of her father's holdings. The man was worth billions. Vultures would be swooping in wanting money, especially with his health failing.

An ache spread through her chest. People were picking away at her father. He was still alive, he was still in control of his will, and all of these people vying for a piece of something that didn't belong to them were seriously making her turn into someone she didn't want to be. If anyone, Graham included, wanted a fight, she'd give them one. She would protect her father, especially now, and she had no doubt her sisters would happily join her in the battle.

Eve finished her orange juice and dry toast so she could take her vitamin and keep it down. She'd learned on day one not to take that pill on an empty stomach and lately she was nauseous anyway. Whether from the pregnancy or from the constant roller coaster with the Newport men, she wasn't sure.

But if Graham expected her to show up in court and do dirty work on behalf of his brothers, she expected something in return.

She shot off a quick text to her assistant to reschedule any morning meetings. Eve already knew there were two, but both were with coworkers and could be adjusted. Nobody would second-guess the president's orders.

Once she finished with Rebecca, Eve sent Graham a text demanding an immediate meeting at her house. If he was going to play hardball, then so was she. Maybe he only knew her well in the bedroom, which was fine, but now the proverbial tables had turned. Hell, they hadn't just turned, they'd been flipped completely over.

Eve quickly showered and threw on her favorite crimson suit. The V of the jacket's lapels was just low enough to be sexy, yet high enough to be professional. She was gearing up for battle and she wanted to look her best.

She'd just applied her lip gloss when her doorbell rang. Eve's master suite was on the first floor of her Chicago mansion. Five bedrooms upstairs were available for any guests, but she rarely went up there. Maybe she'd reconsider once the baby came. She wasn't comfortable being on a separate floor from her child. Of course, at first she'd like the bassinet to be in her room so she could be close to her baby for nightly feedings.

Eve paused and pulled in a breath. That was the exact attitude she needed to keep in regards to this baby. A positive attitude, an outlook that planned for a future with her child. Because nothing would go wrong…fate wasn't so cruel as to take away a second child.

Eve gripped the door handle and gave herself a mental pep talk. The second she opened this door, she had to forget Graham was the father of her child and remember he was the man trying to ruin her father.

Opening the door, Eve stepped back and gestured for Graham to come in. They'd never been formal, and perhaps she should've had this chat on neutral territory, but she wanted to be here, on her turf. This was her day to win the battle.

The moment she closed them inside and turned to face him, her body heated. Damn it. Why did he have to slide that sultry gaze over her? When he started to step toward her, Eve held her hands up.

"This isn't a social call."

Her words didn't deter him as he closed the space between them and slid his hands over her waist, down her hips, and pulled her against him.

"I'm not in the mood to talk anyway," he replied with a slight grin.

When he went for her lips, Eve skirted out from his hold. One kiss and she'd be a goner. There was absolutely no room for hormones right now.

"What was that stunt in the paper all about?" she demanded. Certainly mentioning their family drama would douse any desire he had.

Graham shrugged. "The truth was uncovered."

"The truth," she repeated. "You expect me to believe my father has Winchester heirs milling about

Chicago? Sounds too convenient for this news to come out now."

"Our investigator turned up quite a bit on your father." Graham took one step toward her. "I don't want to argue with you about this. You have to see the truth and accept it."

With a very unladylike growl, Eve turned on her Christian Louboutin heels and made her way into the formal living room. This was one of the few rooms left in her home where they hadn't had sex. She had to focus on the fact that, even though she was expecting, this affair might be coming to an end. How could she continue when he was so adamant about destroying her family?

"I know you're trying to look out for the best interest of Carson," she started before he could say a word. "But you have to see it from my point of view, too. This is my father. I know you all hate him. I know he wasn't the nicest man to you guys."

"He's a bastard."

Crossing her arms over her chest, Eve forged on. "He's dying." Those words hurt to say, but she was fighting for him, so remaining strong was the only option. "This is not the time to drag his name through mud in the press."

"Eve—"

"No. If you want me to come to court, you better get your brother and that investigator to back the hell up." Eve hadn't realized she'd stepped forward until the tips of her shoes were touching Graham's. "I will not negotiate."

A corner of his mouth kicked up into a grin. Eve didn't want to give in to the ridiculous schoolgirl flutter in her belly; she couldn't let her emotions take over. She was already personally involved with him, already carrying his child. She had to have some sort of hold on this…what? Relationship? Did they actually have a relationship? Was there a label that could be placed on whatever they were doing?

Not likely. They were both a mess. The only time things ever seemed to be going their way was in the bedroom. Sex had a way of making you think your world was perfectly fine. Then the cold slap of reality hit.

"If you start laughing—"

Graham snaked an around her waist and pulled her in tight. "Wouldn't dream of it."

"Don't kiss me." Did that protest sound weak? "This isn't a good idea."

He nipped at her jawline, traveled up to her ear and whispered, "Feels like a great idea." His hands curved over her backside, pulling her hips into his.

Graham's hands and mouth, his body for that matter, always seemed like the answer. He made her forget everything except for how her body seemed to zing to life. But she couldn't zing, not today.

Eve pressed her palms to his chest and eased back. "No. I won't be distracted by sex. I want your brother to back off the media attacks and insults."

The muscle in his jaw clenched. "Fine."

Narrowing her eyes, Eve shifted from his grasp. "It's that easy? You agree and know he'll just back down?"

Graham shrugged. "He's acting out of hurt, not rage. I can reason with him."

Eve wanted to believe Graham, but she didn't know Brooks very well. All she knew was how much of a mess they'd created with this secret affair. She was a fool to think their actions wouldn't trickle into their families' lives.

She turned, needing to put some space between them. Having him so close was difficult. They never just talked and she wasn't immune to his charm… much as she'd like to be.

But just as she spun away, a wave of dizziness overcame her. The room tilted before her eyes, and she reached out for any stationary surface. Everything seemed to be moving in slow motion, but Eve cringed, waiting for the hard hit to the floor.

At the last minute, her hand went to her stomach just as strong arms wrapped around her torso.

Secure against Graham's chest, Eve kept her eyes shut as she pulled in a shaky breath. The dizziness remained. It was the first time she'd experienced this pregnancy symptom.

"Okay?" he whispered in her ear.

Not really.

Eve patted the hand he had around her. "I'm okay." She hoped. "Just lost my balance."

Opening her eyes, she focused on the chair and eased from Graham's hold to have a seat. Crossing her legs, she wasn't a bit surprised when his gaze landed directly on her bare skin.

"I want to know what Brooks says and if he plans on getting your PI to ease up. You're attacking a dying man."

Graham unbuttoned his black jacket and crouched at her knees. "We're not attacking, Eve. We simply want your father to do what is right for our half brother. Surely you can see that he's entitled."

"My opinion is irrelevant."

Why was her stomach threatening to revolt? She'd been hoping to bypass this common symptom of pregnancy. She'd rather skip straight to that miracle glow so many raved about. Actually, she'd rather skip to the end when her baby was safe and healthy in her arms.

Heat washed over her. That clammy, instantly hot type of feeling that swept through you when you had the flu…or morning sickness apparently. Why now? Why did this have to happen with Graham here?

"I need to get to work," she told him, hoping he'd leave so she could be miserable all on her own. "Text me later after you talk to Brooks."

Graham's hand slid over her knee. "You're looking pale. Are you okay?"

Of course she looked pale. One minute she was fine, the next she felt like death. Why wasn't he leaving so she could battle this on her own? Why did Mr. Always-Polished-and-Sexy have to see her like this? She prided herself on being that sultry vixen he seemed to believe she was. If she tossed her toast on his Ferragamo shoes, she'd totally ruin her image.

"Eve?"

He wouldn't leave until she assured him she was fine. "Just tired," she told him, attempting to hold her head high and show as little weakness as possible, considering.

His brows dipped. "Are you coming down with something?"

Just a child.

If he didn't think she was fine, he'd never get out of here. With all the energy she had left, Eve pushed herself out of the chair, forcing Graham to come to his feet, as well. She ignored his worried look and started toward the open foyer. Time to show her guest the door before she made a complete fool of herself and he figured out she was pregnant. She couldn't tell him just yet.

"I'm running late," she lied. "You let me know how we're going to proceed after you talk to your brother."

As she reached for the door handle, his hand covered hers.

"Don't push me out."

"We both have work." Why was he so close? His familiar cologne enveloped her, but to her surprise, it didn't turn her stomach. His warm breath tickled her cheek, and any other time she'd relish the moment. Now was definitely not that time.

"I mean mentally," he corrected. Taking her by the shoulders he turned her around. "Whatever is going on with your dad, the courts and my brothers doesn't have to affect us."

Eve couldn't help the laughter that bubbled up. "You're a fool if you believe that. It has already affected us. Until today, we've never kept our clothes on when you came here."

His aqua eyes darkened. "I'm more than ready to rip that suit off you."

And he would. Graham didn't make veiled threats or empty promises. Right now, though, sex was not the answer.

Eve reached behind her and turned the doorknob. "You talk to your brother—we'll talk about the suit ripping later."

His eyes darted down to the V of her jacket, then back to her mouth.

"When I come back later, I want you to still have this on."

With a quick, promising kiss that was anything but innocent and sweet, Graham walked out. Eve shut the door at her back and rested against the wood. How could she feel so nauseous and yet still be reacting to this man?

One thing was sure: until she knew where he stood with this whole inheritance issue, and until the ultrasound came back okay, she wasn't telling him anything. They'd continue on as they had been…having sex and pretending the world around them didn't exist.

Three

"Tell me this is your idea and you're not being persuaded by a woman you should consider our enemy."

Graham eyed his brother, hating how much this paternity issue was eating away at them. They both just wanted answers...answers Sutton had, but refused to share. The man was dying. Why was he now choosing to be loyal to Cynthia? He hadn't chosen her years ago, so this sudden burst of emotion was completely out of character.

And Brooks's actions were also out of character. "This isn't you," Graham stated, eyeing his twin. "Being vindictive. I know you're reacting out of frustration and hurt, but attacking Sutton in the media isn't the way to deal with it."

Brooks grabbed a tumbler from behind the bar in his study and poured two fingers of bourbon. Gripping the glass, he stared down at the contents as if weighing his actions. Eve wasn't forcing Graham to do anything. What she said made sense, and Graham knew his brother wasn't a hateful man. Brooks was fair, honest and loyal…quite the opposite of Sutton Winchester.

"Are you sleeping with her?"

The quietly spoken question hovered in the air. Brooks didn't even look up, but Graham felt the punch to the gut just the same as if his brother had shouted the question.

"Are you going to ease off with the media?" Graham countered. "If you want Eve to cooperate, or any her sisters, we can't come at them like we're coming in for the kill."

Graham winced at his poor choice of words considering the state of the old man. But still, Nora, Grace and Eve weren't to blame. They didn't choose to be born to a man as evil and self-righteous as Sutton.

Brooks tipped back the contents and slammed his glass down onto the polished mahogany bar. "You can't be loyal to your lover and to your family. Your promiscuous ways are going to bite you in the ass."

Graham paced across the room to the floor-to-ceiling window overlooking the city below. This penthouse suite was perfect for a bachelor with a busy lifestyle. "I've gotten along just fine in my professional and personal life without your input."

"If you think getting into bed with a Winchester isn't going to do damage to our family, you're even more blindsided by lust than I first thought. Didn't we agree you'd stay away from her?"

Graham fisted his hands at his side. This was his brother, his twin. They were so similar, yet different. Brooks was the outgoing type, the go-getter, the grounded brother. Graham was definitely outgoing and a go-getter, but he also enjoyed a good time, a good woman. He'd been told often that his quiet charm won him cases and had women falling at his feet. He was just fine with that assessment.

But Graham wasn't ready to give up what he and Eve were doing. Why should he? He'd never experienced anything like Eve before and he sure as hell wasn't going to let Sutton Winchester's will come between them. He'd find a way to make everything work, play the peacemaker and get the job done. Isn't that what he excelled at?

"We didn't agree on anything," Graham stated. "Eve and I are adults. I know where my loyalties are and I won't let anything stand in the way of getting Carson what is rightfully his and getting Sutton to tell us the name of our father. But attacking him in the press isn't the way to go. We need to go in with a milder approach, for a stronger impact."

Brooks quirked a brow. "And how do you suggest doing that?"

Pulling in a breath, Graham turned from the window. "Stop the press war and put a hold on the legal proceedings."

Brooks opened his mouth, but Graham lifted his hand. "Leave this to me. We want Sutton to suffer, but not necessarily his daughters. They'll be hurt, but we can make it less of a blow to them. Sutton is still alive, so as long as he is, we go straight to him. Play hardball with him. Introduce the evidence Roman has discovered and let Sutton make a choice. Tell him we'll go to the media with all the facts, and the lineup of women claiming to have a child by him, or he can put Carson in his will as a beneficiary and give him his share. I'm demanding he give us the name of our father no matter what he chooses to do about the other issues. I refuse to back down on that."

Brooks raked his thumb back and forth on his glass of bourbon, considering all the options. Graham knew he could make this work. He knew Eve would see his side so long as they quit attacking her father. Damn, but he admired her loyalty. Graham just wished she didn't have to be so faithful to such a bastard.

"We'll try your way." Brooks came around the bar, leaned an elbow on top and shot Graham a look. "But you better remember what team you're fighting for."

Graham nodded. "I never forget who I'm fighting for. Carson and you are my top priorities."

Brooks nodded. "Good. I have another topic I want to discuss."

"Does it require more bourbon?"

With a shrug, Brooks crossed the room and took a seat on the leather sofa. "I want to talk to Sutton. In person."

Inwardly cringing, Graham glanced toward the ceiling and wondered why he was surprised. Brooks was a man on a mission. He was determined.

"You want to leave the girls out of this, fine. For now," Brooks added, aiming a hard look at his twin. "But the three of us—Carson, you, me—we're going to talk to Sutton. He's growing weaker every day and I know it may be cruel to go to him and put the pressure on, but we have to try."

Their mother had passed just months ago, taking the secret of who fathered them to her grave. Graham had no idea why she didn't tell them. At first, he'd thought for sure Sutton was their father and she'd been afraid, ashamed. But the DNA test had come back, proving Sutton had only fathered Carson, leaving Brooks and Graham confused and hurt.

While they yearned to know who their father was, Graham was elated that old bastard wasn't his. Not to mention the fact that it had left the path wide open to seduce Eve the night of the charity ball for the children's hospital. He'd gotten the results right before the gala. Eve had shown up wearing a body-hugging gold gown. That honey-brown hair she'd piled perfectly on top of her head came tumbling down all around him when he'd finally gotten her to his penthouse. They'd barely survived the cab ride.

"I'll go with you," Graham stated, pulling himself back into the moment. He needed to be strong for his brothers, needed them to know they were a team. "Sutton isn't as strong as he used to be."

Brooks sent a malevolent grin. "That's what I'm counting on."

After a long day, exhaustion finally won. Eve nearly wept as she submerged herself in the soaker tub in her master suite. All the symptoms of her first pregnancy had come back full force: the need to rest at all times, the nausea that slammed into her with no warning, the emotions that were all over the place. Just trying to keep herself in check at work today had been trying. When someone from a newly acquired company in Barcelona offered condolences for Eve's father, she nearly lost it. Thankfully they had only been chatting on the phone and not via video conference because the tears welled up in her eyes and flowed, but Eve managed to clear her throat, offer thanks and keep her tone neutral.

Why were people acting like he was already gone? That was the part that completely gutted her. He was very much alive, though his health was failing.

Her hand slid down through the lavender-scented bubbles to rest on her flat stomach. Babies were a blessing. The innocence they injected into your life couldn't be matched. Eve wanted to tell her father, wanted to be excited about this new life, but first she had to talk to Graham.

Keeping their child from being a victim in this family war was going to be a struggle, but she refused to believe it was impossible. She knew Graham was loyal to his family—that much was obvious. But how would he react to this child? How would he treat her?

She didn't want him to hover, didn't want him to assume she wanted him as a permanent fixture in her life. She had a plan, goals, a career that was taking off better than she'd ever anticipated.

Tears pricked her eyes. She didn't want this career at the expense of her father's health, his life. She'd taken over as president when he could no longer run Elite Industries.

When her cell chimed, Eve jumped. She should've left the thing in her purse, but she'd been carrying it around like a pacifier lately…because one day she'd get the inevitable call about her father.

The cell lay on the edge of the tub surround. Eve glanced at the screen and saw Nora's name. Worried this might have something to do with her dad, Eve dried her hands off on her towel and quickly read the text.

Relief slid through her when she saw it was just a Halloween party invitation. Sounded fun. In terms of costumes, Eve could go as an overworked, worn down, emotional mess. Maybe she could go in her pajamas with bed hair to really play up the part.

Eve shot back a quick reply to tell her sister she'd be there. Asking if Graham could come as her date probably wasn't the smart thing to do.

Wait. Why was she thinking of taking him anywhere as her date? They weren't dating, they were...

Eve dropped her head against her bath pillow and groaned. She didn't know what they were exactly and that's what annoyed her. She had her life all mapped out with color-coded tabs to tell her when and where to do everything. She prided herself on being efficient, planning everything and knowing exactly what was coming her way.

What she hadn't planned on was the onslaught of desire associated with Graham Newport. One look led to another, then to flirting, which was put on hold when they both realized her father had been involved with his mother. The second they knew Sutton wasn't Graham's father, all bets had been off, all warnings from family ignored.

Eve hadn't been able to get Graham alone fast enough that first night after the children's hospital gala, and from the way he practically tore her dress off her, the feeling was mutual.

That had to have been when she got pregnant. She'd only switched her birth control a week before, thinking it was a safe time since she wasn't seeing anyone. They'd been all over each other before condoms were mentioned, but she'd assured him she was on the pill and they'd quickly had the "I'm clean" conversation.

Thinking back now, Eve realized he would blame her for this pregnancy. She'd assured him she was covered, that they were safe. Well, he could blame her all he wanted, so long as this child remained unaffected by any wrath from the Newports.

When her cell chimed again, Eve jerked from her relaxed position. Even though her body was calm and resting, her mind never shut off. She zeroed in on the screen and saw Graham's name this time. Once again, she dried her hands and checked his message, cursing herself for acting like a teenager.

Meet me at my penthouse. 30 min.

Eve gritted her teeth. While some may go for the demanding attitude, she did not. Besides, she was exhausted. If she could sleep in this warm bubble bath and not drown, she would.

Because she didn't want him to think she jumped when he texted, though she did, Eve set her phone back down without replying. There was no reason to pretend that the thought of Graham didn't have her body humming, but now she had to be realistic. She was expecting his child, and she was entering into a battle over her father… Sex couldn't be the main thread that held them together at this point.

Eve closed her eyes for just a moment, needing to push aside all the fears, all the questions, and just relax. Her doctor told her to try to take as much downtime as possible. Even if she could grab five minutes here and there, she would have to for the sake of the baby and her own health.

All too easily she could let her mind drift into the worry of whether she was carrying a healthy baby, but she wanted to focus on the positive. Would she have a boy or a girl? Would her baby have Graham's striking aqua eyes and her honey hair? One thing was for sure—this child would be strong-willed, determined and take charge, all qualities she and Graham possessed.

Eve's mind went to the nursery, and she instantly envisioned Nora and Grace helping her decorate. She could hire a decorator, but this wasn't a kitchen or bathroom job. No, Eve would take a hands-on approach to her baby's room.

The water had cooled, but Eve was still content to just lie there and relax. The quiet of her home was a welcome reprieve. She'd been in meetings all day, had made numerous decisions regarding offices in several different countries. She wasn't one to have idle time, but she had to admit this felt amazing.

She definitely had to listen to her body, and her body was tired and in need of some downtime.

"Eve."

Water sloshed as she jerked and opened her eyes to see Graham standing in the door separating her bedroom from the bath. Her heart beat out of control in her chest. He'd scared the hell out of her.

She blinked, realizing she'd fallen asleep. The water chilled her now and she shivered as she started to get up.

"What are you doing here?" she asked, stepping from the tub to reach for the towel from the heated bar. "How did you get in?"

His eyes raked over her, causing her chills to multiply for a totally different reason. "You were supposed to meet me an hour ago."

Eve wrapped herself in the towel and secured the edge between her breasts. She'd been asleep that long? Maybe she was more tired than she'd thought.

"First, I never agreed to meet you after you demanded it." She crossed her arms, rolling her eyes when his gaze dipped to her cleavage. "Second, you didn't tell me how you got into my house."

One slow step turned into two and suddenly he was in front of her. His fingertips trailed up her bare arms and shivers wracked her body. Without a word, he tipped his head to rake his lips lightly across her jawline. Eve fisted her hands at her sides. She wanted to clutch him and give in to what he was obviously offering, but she had to think with her head, too.

"You smell amazing," he muttered as his mouth continued to explore her skin. "I worried when you didn't show up."

Eve cursed herself when her head tipped back. With this man, she didn't have control over her body. The fact that he worried about her warmed her, but she couldn't think like that. They weren't in a relationship. In fact, last time she'd talked to him, they were more divided than ever.

"Graham." She pushed at his chest. "We can't do this."

Her slight shove did nothing to budge him. Wrapping his arms around her, he met her eyes.

"Brooks and I have an unspoken understanding."

Eve narrowed her gaze, waiting for him to elaborate. "And that's him keeping his investigator out of my family's business?" she asked when it was clear he wasn't going to go into detail.

"He's staying out of this for now. I don't want to talk about my brothers or your father." He nipped at her lips. "Trust me, Eve. I won't hurt you."

Trust him. Oh, how she wished she could. She had a secret she wasn't ready to reveal and *he* wanted *her* trust. And he may not intend to hurt her, but he was hell-bent on destroying her father, which in turn would most definitely hurt her.

With an expert flick, he had her towel open and gliding to the floor before she could stop him. Every intimate encounter before now had been frenzied, frantic, clothes flying and lips exploring. Something about this slow seduction in her bathroom seemed even more…intimate. Were they crossing a line or was she just reading into this?

"Stop thinking," he demanded in a whisper against her ear. "Feel, Eve. Only feel."

As if she had any other choice.

Four

He couldn't touch her, taste her enough. When she hadn't shown, he'd wondered if she was working, but then she hadn't even replied so he'd panicked like some lovestruck fool. Considering he was neither in love, nor a fool, Graham hated how he'd let his imagination run away from him.

But then he'd gotten into her place, using the security code he'd seen her type in one other time, and every worry fled. Seeing her wet in that tub full of disappearing bubbles, he'd had one mission and that was to get his body on hers as soon as possible.

But he wanted to go slow. She looked positively exhausted, not that he'd ever tell her. He wasn't an idiot when it came to women. Something about how vulnerable Eve looked resting in the bath stirred deeper feelings in him that he'd quickly tamped down, but he welcomed the rush of lust and desire.

He wanted her, he needed her and he planned on having her. Now.

Her bathroom was spacious, complete with a vanity island in the middle. Perfect. He scooped her up, sat her on the edge and stepped between her thighs.

Running his hands up her legs, over those rounded hips and over her waist, Graham wasn't surprised when she trembled beneath his touch. Trembling was a nice start, but he planned on having her writhing, panting his name.

Her fingers curled around his shoulders. "We shouldn't do this anymore," she argued, but her words came out on a whisper, betraying her true feelings.

Graham slid one fingertip between her breasts and down to her abdomen. "And why is that?"

Eve sucked in a breath as her lids lowered. Yes. That was the reaction he wanted to see. Complete surrender.

"B-because. We want…"

Graham leaned forward, his mouth trailing along the path his finger had just traveled. "Oh, yes. We want."

Her hands framed his face as she urged him back up to look at her. "We want different things," she stated, her eyes holding on to his.

"Right now I'd say we want the exact same thing."

"It's not in here that I'm worried about."

She had every reason to worry, but he meant it when he said he wouldn't hurt her. Eve was innocent, but she may feel some of the aftershock of her father's wrath. Everything that was coming down on them was a result of Sutton's actions. If anyone was hurting Eve, it was her father. Couldn't she see that?

"I told you to trust me," Graham reminded her. His hand settled between her thighs. "No more talking."

The second he touched her, she moaned. Leaning back on her hands, she offered herself up exactly the way he'd been fantasizing about all day. He'd wanted her in his penthouse with the city lights flooding into his living room, but this was fine, too. If anyone stopped by to visit, they wouldn't see his car because she'd given him a bay in the second garage in the back of the house for such eventualities. This sneaking around only amped up his desire. Graham never backed away from a challenge and he damn well wouldn't start now that Eve was having doubts.

The more his hand moved over her center, the more she let out those sexy little moans. Then she'd bite her lip as if she hadn't meant to show how much she enjoyed what they were doing.

He wanted to bite that lip.

Graham continued stroking her as he leaned forward and took her mouth with his. She instantly opened to him, matching his need with her own. And that's what made Eve so perfect in the bedroom.

They had the exact same needs, they knew how to pleasure each other without a single word and neither of them expected anything beyond exactly this.

Eve tore her mouth away and shut her eyes as her entire body tightened. Watching her come undone was the sexiest experience of his entire life. She had no qualms about the noises she made, or the way her damp hair clung to the side of her cheek when she'd thrown her head to the side. This was Eve. His Eve.

No. Not his. She would never be his. This was temporary, no more.

The moment her body relaxed, Graham jerked her to the edge of the counter and unfastened his pants. He couldn't wait another minute. He needed to have her and didn't want her coming off the high she'd just had. She was everything he needed at this exact moment, and he refused to look beyond that. There was no future…not for them.

Her arms wrapped around his neck, her breasts pressed up against his dress shirt and he didn't even care that he was still technically fully clothed. That was the need he had for this woman.

Eve's ankles locked behind him and Graham bent his head to claim that precious mouth once more as he joined their bodies.

Would he ever get enough of her? He kept waiting for this new sensation to wear off, but it had been several weeks now and he was just as achy for her as ever. There was a desire inside him that he hadn't known before her. Part of him wondered if they'd still sneak around if their families weren't the Newports and the Winchesters.

When Eve arched her back, pulling her mouth from his, he took the opportunity to capture one perfect breast with his lips. His actions were rewarded with another soft moan as she gripped his shoulders. Her body quickened the pace, and he was all too eager to join her.

When she cried out his name, it was the green light he needed from her to follow her over the edge. He held her as they trembled together, held her after their bodies had cooled and then carried her into her bed.

And Graham refused to even think about why he was feeling so protective of her right now. This had nothing to do with Sutton, Brooks or Carson. His actions had nothing to do with how worn she'd looked when he'd arrived.

No, this was only sex. Nothing more. It couldn't be.

Eve finished the conference call with one of her father's established clients in Miami. Even though she was taking Elite Industries into global territory, there was still a need to keep the current clients satisfied. Now that Eve was president, she intended to not only continue building on current relationships, but also adding to their Elite family. This business was all she'd known; she was molded to fill this role and she took every bit of it seriously.

Eve popped in another peppermint and willed the

flavor to calm her queasy stomach. She'd read from multiple sites—and her doctor had confirmed—that peppermint would alleviate the queasiness.

Two days had passed since Graham had shown up in her bathroom. Two days since she'd had the opportunity to tell him about the baby. But there was that whole family rivalry standing between them, driving the wedge deeper with each passing day. Graham had urged her to trust him, but that word was too easily thrown around. And what had he meant by that? He'd implored her at her weakest moment, and damn if she hadn't given in.

She wanted to trust him in more areas than just her body. She had to believe that he'd taken care of getting Brooks to stay away from the media. Dirty rumors could damage her family's reputation. Something that would start a domino effect and impact Elite Industries.

She refused to allow Graham, Brooks or Carson to destroy the only life she'd ever known. The life she needed to secure for her child.

A light tap on her door had Eve straightening in her seat. Shoving the peppermint into the side of her mouth, she called, "Come in."

The door swung open and Eve's younger sister, Nora, stepped in. Nora in all her beauty and radiance. She'd fallen in love with hotelier Reid Chamberlain and the two were deliriously happy. Reid had also taken to Nora's son and they were absolutely adorable together. Over the past several weeks, the trio had become inseparable. Eve was thrilled to see her sister find her soul mate. Being a single mother had to be so difficult, but Nora had always made life look like a breeze.

The tug on Eve's heart had her cursing herself. She wasn't jealous. Jealousy meant she wanted love, a man in her life. She didn't need, nor did she want those things. Staying focused on Elite, and now this precious baby she carried, was all she had time for. Being a single mom would be difficult, but women did it every single day and, damn it, Eve wouldn't fail. She refused to be intimidated by her fears.

"I hope you're not busy." Nora slid her plaid scarf from around her neck and dropped it, and her designer purse, onto the chair across from Eve's desk. "I was out and wanted to swing by. I haven't seen you in a few days."

Eve pasted a smile on her face. "I've been busy. I got your text about the party."

Nora beamed. "You have to be there, Eve. Grace won't tell me her costume but swears it's going to be awesome. Reid and I are thinking of either going as a Viking couple or as Superman and Lois Lane."

"Sounds fun."

Nora tipped her head to the side. "You're bringing a date, right?"

Everything inside Eve stilled. A date. Probably not, considering that she'd only been with Graham for the past six weeks. Plus, they weren't dating, not by any means. And with the way things were going in the press, there was no way in hell a Newport would be allowed inside a Winchester's home. Well, Eve's home didn't count, but her sisters would never stand for Eve and Graham being an item.

Eve cringed. An item? They'd never been on a date. They snuck around, they'd created a child and now she had to figure out a way to tell him, considering they were definitely *not* an item. So, no. No date for her at the party.

"I've been a little too busy to date." Too busy sneaking in time between the sheets with a Newport. "But I promise I'll be there in costume."

Nora rolled her eyes and dropped onto the other leather chair. "You work too hard, Eve. You need to date. There's not one man you can ask to be your date?"

Well, there was a man, but…

"I don't need a date," Eve stated, propping her elbows on her desk. "I'm happy for you and Reid, but not all of us want that happily-ever-after. I'm building Elite and taking it into the next generation. It's not easy work, so I haven't had much social life."

Okay, two days ago she'd done social life right on the vanity in her bathroom, but that wasn't necessary to point out here.

A solemn look instantly came over Nora's face. "Have you been to see Dad in the past couple days?"

Guilt ate away at Eve. She'd been busy building this company he'd left in her care. She wanted him to see how far she could take it before he…passed.

But thinking about the inevitable had tears burning her eyes.

"I know," Nora whispered, swiping at her own eyes. "I'm on my way there, actually. Grace was there last night and said he was having a good day. I hope he's still the same when I get there."

Their father was in his home being nursed by the best caregivers they could find. He was a man of dignity; he didn't want his last days to be in a nursing home or hospital and Eve couldn't blame him. She and her sisters were just fine with granting him any wish he had right now.

"Have you seen Carson?" Nora asked.

Blinking away the tears, Eve shook her head. "I haven't."

Their new half brother. To find out after all this time they had a brother was definitely a blow. Sutton had been known to have affairs, or so the rumor mill had spun it over the past several years, but now there was proof. Eve wasn't quite sure how to handle Carson, but she did know he didn't deserve any of her father's holdings. He knew nothing of her father. They shared DNA only. There was no bond, there were no treasured moments. Not that any of that was Carson's fault, but Eve wasn't ready to embrace him just yet. And she certainly wasn't ready to argue over her father's assets while he was still alive.

"He's requested to see father."

Eve straightened. "What?"

"He wants to talk," Nora clarified. "We can't deny him, Eve. He has every right to see his father."

Before he dies. The unspoken words hovered between them, driving home the point that their father was human. He'd cheated on their mother, now he was dying. He shouldn't have to keep paying for his sins, and he shouldn't have his name tarnished when his days were numbered.

And that brought Eve's thoughts right back to Graham. Was Carson requesting to see their father because he was trying to gain ammunition for their media campaign? Every protective instinct welled up inside her.

"It's a bad idea," Eve told her sister. "He could be plotting with Brooks and Graham."

"I don't think that's what he's doing. Brooks hired a private investigator. If they want to dig up Dad's past, we can't stop them and I highly doubt Dad will give up any skeletons in his closet on his own at this point."

Nora's words sank in, and actually made sense. Still…

Graham had wanted her to trust him. Those words kept bouncing back and forth in her head and she truly wished she knew what the answer was.

"What does Grace think?" Eve asked.

Nora lifted a slender shoulder. "She's fine with letting Carson in. She's not as cynical as you are, though."

"I prefer the term *realistic*," Eve countered. With

a heavy sigh, she nodded. "Fine. But one of us needs to be in the room."

Nora nodded. "I agree. I'll let Carson know and we can set up a time."

"Wait." Eve pressed her palms to her desk and eased back in her seat. "Have you asked Dad?"

"He wants to see his son."

Those simple words were what this all boiled down to. Carson was Sutton's son. The final say belonged to their father and he would never turn away family…especially a newly discovered son.

"Let me know when and I'll make sure I'm there," Eve told her sister.

Nora got to her feet and pulled her scarf back around her neck. After adjusting her navy cardigan, she grabbed her handbag and hooked the strap on her forearm.

"Try not to work so hard," Nora said, a soft, caring tone lacing her voice. "You're looking tired and you have assistants who can help."

Eve laughed. "Wow, thanks for the confidence booster."

Circling the desk, Nora embraced her. "I say this because I love you. Don't let work rule your life like Dad did. Take time for yourself. Who knows? You may change your mind about that happily-ever-after but find your Prince Charming has passed you by while you were stuck in your office."

Graham's face instantly came to mind, but he was far from Prince Charming. He was more the evil villain with charm and charisma that made him impossible to resist. Besides, she didn't need anyone to rescue her—prince or peasant.

"I promise to get more rest," Eve assured her as she eased back. "Now, go on and see Dad. Tell him I'll be by later."

Once Nora was gone, Eve fell back into her seat. She was exhausted, and it was showing. She was going to have to take better care of herself. Her life wasn't just about her anymore. She had an innocent child to care for, and she would do anything to keep her child safe.

Reliving the nightmare of losing a baby wasn't an option. But fear had a crippling hold over her. Between the worry of miscarriage and telling Graham, she had some legitimate concerns. Would this be a replay of the last time? Granted, before she'd thought herself in love. She wasn't as naive this time. But she still wanted Graham to be accepting of their child, wanted him to take part in the baby's life.

She had to tell him. Tonight. There was no easy way to drop this bomb and she wasn't a coward. No matter what happened after she told him, she'd be just fine.

Five

She'd avoided him for two days. Two. Damn. Days.

Graham had gone to bat for her, going against his brothers, and Eve had dodged his texts and calls. The fact that he'd thrown away all common sense when Eve had pleaded with him to not ruin her father spoke volumes. That's something someone in a relationship would do. They weren't in a relationship. They had sex. Private, sneaking-around, amazing sex.

Well, they had been. But when he'd been at her place and they'd been intimate, she'd turned down any further advances the morning after. Did she want to call this affair quits? Too bad. He wasn't ready and her body's response to his touch told him otherwise. Not that he would beg. Hell, no. And he didn't want a relationship, but he certainly wasn't ready to end this.

Even if he wanted something more, he was too swamped with being a partner in his law firm to feed any type of relationship. Sex was a stress reliever and Eve was definitely on the same page, though she may have been fighting herself on this matter. She was just as vigilant in her career and wanted nothing more. So, when she ignored his texts, it shouldn't have bothered him…but it did. Eve wasn't one to play games, and if she wanted to put on the brakes, he imagined that she'd just tell him so.

Then, as if she hadn't been silent for two days, she texted him to say she needed to talk.

He didn't like the sound of that. The whole we-need-to-talk thing was such a veiled subject and he didn't like how it eluded to the fact that she may want to call this quits.

Eve possessed every quality he'd ever wanted in a lover. She was career driven—so she wasn't monopolizing his time—she was passionate and damn if she didn't challenge him…in bed and out.

He'd never cared when another woman blew off his calls, though that rarely happened. The few times it had, he'd moved on. No worries. Yet with Eve, he wasn't going to have her call it quits without seducing her one last time. If she wanted to move on, he wouldn't stop her, but he sure as hell would give her a send-off she'd never forget.

Just the thought of getting his hands on her again had Graham hurrying to get to her office. He'd purposely waited until it was good and dark before setting out. With the skies darkening earlier this time of year, he was able to log in more hours with her.

Damn. He shouldn't keep track of the hours he'd spent with her. He should be going with the flow in this casual hookup arrangement. But he was human and Eve turned him on like no one else ever had. So what if he wasn't ready to put the brakes on just yet?

Graham wasn't oblivious to the fact that he hadn't seen anyone else since that night at the ball when he'd seduced Eve. Had he ever gone this long with the same woman? Other women would think things were getting serious, but not Eve. She knew the boundaries. Besides, even if they wanted to make this something more permanent, no way in hell would their family feud allow that to happen. The last thing he wanted was his brothers or her sisters in their business.

No, it was all about sneaking and seducing. That was the name of the game. He'd been looking for a label and he'd found one. Simple as that.

So what if he had a designated bay in her second garage all to himself. He refused to believe this was serious. Hiding his car when he visited her at her house was merely precautionary, that was all. If one of her sisters or assistants stopped by, he could easily hide in one of the rooms of her sprawling mansion. A car would be a bit harder to explain if it was out in the open.

But now he was at her office, parking in a public garage, so there. Why the hell was he arguing with himself? He'd rather concentrate on Eve and how quickly he could have her on her desk panting his name. Ironically, she was the perfect distraction from the investigation and beating his head against the wall where Sutton was concerned.

Graham took the elevator up to her office. Nobody would be there this time of the evening, and Eve wouldn't have requested he come if her assistant or any other staff members were hanging around. Their offices had quickly become the go-to choice for late-night rendezvous.

As he made his way down the wide, tiled hall, the intense, familiar scent of Eve's jasmine perfume enveloped him. Would he ever tire of smelling it? When she'd wrapped herself around him after her bubble bath the night before last, he'd inhaled that sweet scent. Everything about Eve was a punch to his gut. The desire for her hadn't lessened one bit—if anything, he only craved her more. That was dangerous territory to venture into, but he was in complete control. He had to be.

Her office door was slightly cracked, a sliver of light slashing the dark floor tiles. Without bothering to knock or give a warning, he pushed open the door and found her at her computer. As Graham moved closer, he realized she was staring at her screen, scrolling with her mouse, but she didn't seem to be focusing in on any one thing.

She hadn't said a word, hadn't even turned to acknowledge his presence. As he came behind her chair, he glanced at the screen. Photo after photo of Eve with her sisters and their father in various places and times continued to scroll up the monitor. Sometimes she'd stop, scroll back down, then commence to go up again. Eve was a brilliant photographer. The images around the entire floor of her office proved that. She claimed her photography was a hobby, but he knew full well if she ever opted out of the real estate industry, she could turn pro without fail.

Graham swallowed. Whatever she'd called him here for had to do with that old bastard. Talk about a mood killer.

When she didn't say anything, Graham surveyed her spacious office overlooking the city. The floor-to-ceiling windows showed off a brilliant Chicago skyline dotted with lights. As he turned, he noted the built-in bookshelves on the far wall were full of books, mostly on photography and real estate. When Eve was passionate about something, she put her whole self into it. He could attest to that.

But the fact that he admired and cared about her hobbies was even more dangerous than having his physical desire escalate. Getting too personal meant setting down roots. He wasn't about to set down roots with any woman. Ever. Let alone a woman whose family bitterly rivaled his.

Graham walked back to the desk, setting his hip on the edge beside her chair. The picture she'd homed in on now was of a smiling Sutton surrounded by his daughters. This had to have been taken recently. Eve wore that killer red suit she'd had on a few days ago and Sutton wasn't looking well. But he actually smiled in these pictures. Graham didn't want to see his old rival as a human being capable of such emotions.

"I'm almost done," she told him, without turning. "I have a few more to upload."

Graham didn't want to see Sutton's face on the screen another second, especially not with Eve smiling back from the picture. Guilt twisted the knife in his chest. He had no right to hate the relationship between Eve and her father. He had no right to… what? Be jealous? No way was he jealous. That was absolutely…

Damn it. Maybe he was jealous. How did a man like Sutton deserve love and loyalty from someone so caring and trusting as Eve? Sutton was a bastard and that he'd managed to raise three amazing women was a miracle.

Sutton may have been a conniving jerk, but he'd made the right choice putting Eve in charge of his company. There was no one better to run Elite Industries. She had a vision, something fresh that would drive the company into the next several decades. She was brilliant, independent and charming. She had all the traits that would make Elite expand in the exact ways she wanted it to because she refused to take no for an answer, and she refused to fail.

"I saw my father today." Her soft words cut into the silence. "Grace and Nora happened to be there at the same time. Dad knows I always have my camera on hand, so he wanted family pictures in case..."

Graham didn't like that vulnerable, lost tone in her voice. Selfish as Graham was, and as much as he loathed Sutton, he wasn't going to let Eve grieve alone. The loss of a parent was still too fresh, too painful for him. Nobody should have to face such emptiness on their own.

Squatting down beside her chair, he gripped the arms and turned her to face him. Finally, her bright green gaze landed on his. "It's good you have these pictures. Many family members don't get to say goodbye, let alone capture the final memories."

Moisture gathered in her eyes as she nodded. When one lone tear slipped down her cheek, Graham reached to swipe it away. But his hand lingered on her cheek, his thumb sliding across the darkness beneath her eye.

"You're tired," he said before he could catch himself. "Maybe you should go home and rest."

"I'm fine. It's only seven. I wouldn't sleep now, anyway."

Stubborn. Hardheaded. So much like himself, he felt as if he were looking in a mirror. Still, he wouldn't let her work herself to death and that had nothing to do with their intimacy. He wouldn't want to see anyone this exhausted and worn down.

"What time did you come in today?"

She pursed her lips and looked away. "I think five. Or maybe it was five yesterday and six today. I can't remember right now."

He clenched his teeth and counted backward from ten. She was pushing herself too hard and someone needed to intervene.

"You have spreadsheets scheduling your bathroom breaks at work and you can't recall when you came in or how long you worked today?"

Eve's sharp gaze collided with his. "So?"

"You're working too hard. You're going to break if you don't slow down."

Narrowing her eyes, Eve stood up, but Graham didn't get out of her way. "That's the second time today someone has said that to me. My apologies if I look tired. I'm in negotiations with a company we want to take over, my sister is pressuring me to bring a date to some silly costume party and my father is dying. I'll try to look less exhausted tomorrow and double up on concealer."

Her words sank in and Graham got to his feet and reached up to cup her shoulders. Closing the miniscule gap between them, he brought her body flush against his.

"I'll be your date." Because no way in hell was another man going on her arm.

Eve blinked away her unshed tears. "You can't be

my date. Nora and Reid are hosting the party at my dad's. You think they're just going to let a Newport onto the Winchester estate?"

Graham shrugged. "I'll wear a mask and a great costume. Introduce me as whoever you want. But I'm your date."

"No," she said with a shake of her head. "I'll go alone."

So long as no schmuck was escorting her, Graham was fine. Still, part of him wanted to go with her, but she was right: that was ridiculous thinking. They weren't a couple, so why pretend to be one? He hated how his instant go-to idea was to be with her as her date. They didn't date. Sneaking around after dark, parking their cars where they couldn't be seen and sending texts in code was not dating.

Circling back around to the original topic, Graham asked, "What are you doing to yourself?" Sliding his thumbs beneath her eyes, he let out a sigh.

Eve blinked but remained silent. Something was going on with her. He wasn't sure what, but he wasn't leaving until he knew. Maybe it was the stress from her father's illness and from buying another company, just as she'd said. But could it be something else?

"If you want to end things, just say so."

Her eyes widened as she shifted back slightly. "What?"

Graham dropped his hands. He couldn't touch her and not want her, but he'd be damned if he begged.

"If you want to bring this arrangement to a close, that's fine."

The color drained from her face. She started to step back, but hit her chair and lost her balance. Graham reached around to grab her, but she pushed away. Struggling out of his hold, she ended up moving around him and putting a good bit of distance between them.

"That's fine?" she repeated. "If you're that detached from this…whatever this is, then leave."

Careful of his next words, Graham slid his hands into his pockets. Eve was clearly on edge and his blasé words hadn't helped. He hadn't expected her to be so upset. Still, this was useful information to have. Clearly she wasn't calling him here to break things off.

He closed the gap between them, following her when she took two more steps back. Those expressive green eyes remained locked onto his, but her never-ending steely determination had her jaw clenched, her nostrils flaring.

"I'm not leaving," he finally replied. She may try to be fierce, but she looked as if she'd break at any moment. "Tell me why you called me here."

She blinked once, then shook her head. "It can wait."

When she attempted to skirt him once more, Graham reached out to grip her biceps. "Stop running. Tell me, Eve. I haven't heard from you in two days and I haven't felt you beneath me in just as long. What's going on if you're not ending things?"

She continued to stare at him as she bit the inside of her cheek. Whatever she was gearing up to tell him must be something major. Obviously she wasn't going to tell him to take a hike, but what else was there? Did she have news on Sutton she was afraid to share?

Eve pulled in a shaky breath, her body trembling beneath his hands. She was scared. Whatever was going on had her terrified because he'd never seen Eve this run-down, this unsure of her words.

"Just tell me," he stated, sounding harsher than he intended. "My mind is spinning and I have no clue what you want to tell me."

"I've rehearsed this in my head, but now that you're here, I can't find the words."

Worry coursed through him. They may not be a serious item, but Graham wanted to reassure her he wasn't some unfeeling ass. He framed her face and nipped at her lips.

"Whatever you need to tell me, we'll deal with it. Are you sick? Is it something with your dad you think I won't care about? What, Eve?"

Her dark lashes rested against her cheeks as she let out a sigh. Finally, she lifted her lids, and her eyes locked onto his.

"I'm pregnant."

Six

Graham didn't release her. He couldn't even think, so getting his brain in gear to let go wasn't happening.

Pregnant. How could one word cause such panic and uncertainty? And why did this room seem to be closing in on him?

His hands fell from her arms. Graham raked his fingers through his hair and attempted to pull his scattered thoughts together. Over the past six weeks they'd been intimate so many times. He had no idea when this had happened. All he recalled was that first time when they'd been in such a rush and she'd assured him she was on birth control.

"Say something," she whispered.

"Did you plan this?"

Eve jerked as if she'd been slapped by his words. "I would never do that."

Graham shrugged. "How do I know? Despite the past month and a half, I don't know you that well."

Eve's cheeks pinkened with rage the instant before her hand came up in a flash and struck his face. The crack seemed to echo in the open office. Graham's head jerked, but he didn't reach up to touch the sting.

"You can't blame me for asking," he countered, refusing to feel sympathy despite the hurt in her eyes. "I assume this baby is mine."

Her eyes narrowed. "I haven't been with anyone else since we started seeing each other."

He firmly believed that. Eve was too busy at work for fun and he occupied her evenings, save for the past couple. Still, a paternity test would be required considering he had quite a padded bank account. Someone like Eve wouldn't be after a man's money, though. But he would be smart about this. And being smart, he wouldn't bring up the test right now or his other cheek may feel the same sting.

"I don't expect anything from you," she went on, crossing her arms over her chest. "In fact, maybe we should bring what's between us to a close and focus on what's best for the baby."

Graham didn't know what he wanted right now. His entire world had been flipped and control had never been so out of his reach. But he didn't want to just end things with Eve, especially now.

"That won't change the situation." Graham struggled to keep his distance, but he needed to play his cards right. "I will be here every step of the way, Eve. Whether you want me around or not. This child is a Newport and I never turn my back on my responsibilities."

"Is that what I am now?" she asked. "A responsibility?"

So maybe he hadn't chosen his words as wisely as he'd intended. "You're the mother of my child."

He watched her shoulders relax as relief slid over her. But then Eve blinked and her gaze darted away. Was she worried he'd reject her and the child? Didn't she know him at all?

Of course she didn't. He'd even thrown that fact in her face moments ago. They truly didn't know each other. And now they were going to be parents.

Brooks and Carson were going to…hell, he didn't know what their reaction would be. But for now, he was keeping this information to himself.

What would Sutton say? Once the man found out his responsible daughter was pregnant by his enemy, would he change his mind and give up the secrets he was keeping about Graham and Brooks's paternity? A plan started forming in Graham's mind.

"Have you told your sisters?"

Eve shook her head. "I haven't told anyone. I… I'm not sure they'll take this very well."

Most likely not. And he knew Sutton wouldn't take it well, either. The man probably had higher hopes for his daughter and new president of Elite Industries than having a child by a Newport. But Graham was serious when he said he'd be there through everything. He may not have planned on having a child with anyone, let alone Eve, but he would never turn his back on an innocent child... especially his own.

A possessive streak shot through him as he stared back at Eve. This was why she looked so tired, why she was likely running herself ragged. She was scared of the pregnancy, worried about the backlash when the rest of their world discovered the truth. Again, he would be there. Nobody would hurt his child or the child's mother, no matter what their relationship status was.

"Let's keep this between us until we know how to deliver the news."

Eve nodded. Her arms went around her waist, as if to somehow protect their child. "I don't want our baby to receive backlash from either of our families. No matter what's going on or not going on between you and me, please promise me you'll protect our child."

The urgency in her tone had Graham stepping toward her. "I promise."

The vow came easily because he'd walk through hell to keep his child safe. Odd how he'd only known about this baby for mere minutes and already his priorities had changed. And one thing was certain: his child would have his last name, even if he had to marry Eve.

The idea made him cringe. Not that being married to Eve would be terrible, but he didn't want to be married to anybody. Still, some marriages were made of lesser things. At least he and Eve understood the importance of each other's work and they would both love this child.

"When is your doctor's appointment? I want to go."

Eve shook her head. "That isn't necessary."

"I'm going."

Chewing on her bottom lip, she nodded. "Fine. It's next week. I went the other day for initial blood work. He said everything looked fine and gave me vitamins and my due date."

As Graham listened to her, he was already thinking about the time when the baby would arrive. All work would have to be put on hold. No way in hell was he missing the birth of his child.

His child.

Unable to stop himself, Graham reached out and eased her arms aside before placing his flat palm against her stomach. To even think there was a life growing inside of her, a life he'd helped create, absolutely humbled him.

Eve stilled beneath him. When he glanced up to her face and caught sight of her wide eyes, he swallowed and stepped back.

"I have no idea how to act," he admitted, shoving his hands in his pockets. "I don't want to upset you, but I want you to be aware how serious I'm going to take this."

"Honestly, I just want to figure out how to make sure our families won't turn against us or this child. That's all I care about. Anything between us doesn't matter anymore."

A point he wholeheartedly disagreed with, but his actions would speak for him over time. He wasn't going anywhere, and keeping Eve close would be simple. No way was another man moving in. Eve and this child were his. Period.

Graham made sure that if there was something he wanted, nothing stood in his way. He may not want a family in the traditional sense, but letting Eve just put up a barrier between them was out of the question. His desire for her hadn't diminished one bit. In fact, knowing she carried his child was the biggest turn-on he'd ever experienced.

"How are you feeling?" He hadn't even asked her. He'd jumped straight into wondering if she'd trapped him, to asking about paternity, to wanting to feel her still-flat stomach.

"Fine."

The clenched half smile betrayed her. Graham tipped his head. "You can't lie to me, Eve. You're exhausted—you admitted that earlier. But how else are you feeling? Does the doctor think you can keep working all these crazy hours or should you be resting?"

She stared at him, not answering, not even attempting to answer. Her eyes welled up once again and Graham waited. What had he said wrong? He had a million questions, but right now he wanted to know how she was feeling.

"I know this is your child, but…" Eve's words died away as she turned her back to him. Graham reached for her shoulders, but pulled back at the last minute.

The only sound in the room was Eve's shaky breathing. The lights of the Chicago skyline spilled in from the window. They'd shared some intense experiences in this office, but nothing compared to the intensity of this moment.

"Why do you care?" she whispered.

"Because you're carrying a Newport." Damn, that sounded heartless. Why was that his first response? Why did he have to sound so cold?

Because he couldn't let himself feel anything else for Eve. He had to remain detached. Their families made the Montagues and the Capulets look like besties and he couldn't cross the emotional boundary with her. Granted, having a child together was crossing the point of no return, but that didn't mean they had to set up and play house together. Plenty of children had parents who didn't live together. Whatever the arrangement, Graham wouldn't let his child ever want for love, stability or a solid foundation.

Squaring her shoulders, Eve turned and swiped her damp cheeks. "Well, I have some emails to send. I'll text you all the specifics about my doctor's appointment, but if anyone sees us coming and going—"

"You're dismissing me?" Unbelievable.

Her eyes didn't hold the heat or the light he was used to seeing. Now she stared at him as if he were merely a business associate. "I have work. Surely you understand."

"I understand you're trying to keep some ridiculous wall between us." Anger bubbled within him. He didn't know what he wanted her to do or say, but he sure as hell didn't want this unfeeling Eve. "I'll be at the damn appointment if I have to sneak in the back way."

Eve nodded and moved around him to settle back in at her desk. She wiggled her mouse until her screen came back to life. And right there was Sutton's face smiling back, with his hand holding Eve's. Graham had not only been dismissed, he was being mocked by a man who wasn't even in the room.

"We'll talk later," he promised, heading toward the door. "Don't believe for one second this changes what we had going, Eve. I still want you, and if you're honest, you want me, too. That passion isn't something that can be turned off."

Her hands froze as she gave him a sidelong glance.

"I'll give you the space you want," he went on,

gripping the door handle. "But you better get ready because I won't be far and I won't wait long."

With that vow, Graham stormed out. *Game on.* Graham wasn't concerned about how their families would react to the baby. He refused to allow anything other than complete and utter love and acceptance. No, what Graham needed to concentrate on was the fact he wasn't done with Eve, in the personal sense that had nothing to do with their child.

And if she thought he was going to walk away from her or their child, well, she was about to find out that a Newport always got what he wanted.

Seven

"What the hell is wrong with you?" Carson threw his cards down onto the green felt and leaned back in his seat. "You're moping like a woman."

Graham wasn't in the mood for company, let alone playing poker and chatting with his brothers. But when Carson had stopped by earlier, he'd apparently picked up on Graham's doldrums right away and called for reinforcements, texting Brooks to come, as well. Now here they all were.

Graham proudly laid down his royal flush and raked in the chips. Maybe he wasn't in the mood, but he'd been on a winning streak. After sorting the chips by color and putting them away, Graham got to his feet and took his empty tumbler back to the built-in bar.

"I'm done here." Graham refilled his glass with his favorite bourbon. "I'll go put on *The Maltese Falcon*."

They had an ongoing tradition that stretched back to a time when they lived with their mother and Gerty. Gerty introduced them to the Hollywood classics and insisted they watch them together. To this day, they continued to honor her tradition.

Graham missed her. She was a strong woman, a woman who refused to let life knock her down, and she'd do anything to help others. His mother had been just as strong. A lump formed in his throat as he slid his fingers over the remote to start the movie. Each day seemed to be better than the last, but he knew he'd always feel the void from the loss of Gerty and his mother.

Graham had so many questions now that his mother was gone. She'd been single, pregnant and scared when she'd come to Chicago. Had she even told Graham and Brooks's father that they existed? Had he knowingly turned his back on her or did he have no clue he'd fathered twin boys?

These were questions Graham may never have an answer to. Cynthia took her secrets to her grave. The truth would be something he and Brooks would have to uncover all on their own. At least they had ruled out Sutton as their father, which was a blessing in itself. But the bastard knew the truth and was dodging them. His time was limited, which meant that Graham had to take drastic action if he wanted answers.

The idea of using Eve to obtain the information had his stomach in knots, but she was carrying his child and if Graham had to let that news slip to Sutton in order to get information…well…

Graham heard his brothers behind him as they came into the home theater. But his mind wasn't on the movie or even the idea of his father out in the world somewhere. His mind was on Eve. The parallel between her and his mother's experiences wasn't lost on him, but there was a huge difference. Graham planned on being part of this child's life. Eve wouldn't be alone, she wouldn't have to worry about facing this without support.

"He's still got that look," Brooks muttered. "He won every damn hand and still looks like he's ready to punch the wall."

"Your face would do," Graham replied without glancing over. "I like my walls intact."

"If you're going to fight, at least pause the movie," Carson interjected. "I know we just watched this one a few weeks ago, but it's still my favorite."

Graham shook the ice cubes around in his glass. "I'm not going to hit anything, but if you two keep discussing my mood, I'm likely to change my mind."

Graham turned the volume up until the surround-sound speakers hidden around the room were blaring. He'd had enough of the chitchat and getting in touch with his feelings.

There was no mention of Sutton tonight, which was a relief. Brooks had his PI on the hunt for their father, and apparently there was still no news. Maybe they could just have a regular night like they used to. Something bland and boring. Graham never thought he'd wish for such a thing, but lately his life seemed to be heading in about twelve different directions.

His cell vibrated in his pocket. Setting his glass on the table next to his theater recliner, Graham slid the phone out and held it down to his side so his brothers couldn't see. The screen lit up with Eve's name. He wasn't going to reach out to her just yet. He wanted to leave her wondering when he'd be back, when he'd make a move. There was an ache in him that drove him insane and he wanted her to be just as achy, just as needy.

He quickly read her message.

Dr. McNamera November 17 9:00

That was all. Nothing more, nothing personal. The dynamics of their relationship had changed. Because he was apparently a masochist, he scrolled through their previous messages. Flirting, hookup times, codes for what they would do to each other once they were alone. He shifted in his seat as he recalled doing exactly those things.

It was late, but that didn't mean she wasn't at her office. She worked even on weekends, not that he could fault her because he knew that drive to stay on top of the career you'd worked so hard for. But he wanted to see her, needed to see her.

For the first time in…ever, Graham willed this movie to end. He loved spending time with his brothers, valued their special bond, but right now he had other plans.

Plans that involved Eve, a dark room and no interruptions from the outside world. He didn't want her to get swept away into the fear of being pregnant. He wanted her relaxed and he knew exactly how to make that happen.

Intending to make it through the next couple hours, Graham opted not to refill his bourbon. Two glasses were enough because he wanted his head on straight.

"You all up for more poker?" Brooks asked as the credits rolled.

"I need to get home," Carson replied, coming to his feet. "I don't have to spend my nights looking at you two anymore."

Carson had found love. Good for him. Graham wasn't jealous, he just didn't believe in such things. Still, whatever Carson and Georgia had together was genuine. The way they looked at each other, the way they were always looking out for the other was a testament to their deep bond.

"Can't say I blame you," Brooks countered. "You're a lucky man."

Brooks wanted that home life. He wanted the wife, the kids, all of that. Graham wanted to nail this case he was working on and get Eve to come around to seeing they didn't need to cool it in the sheets simply because they'd created a child. "I actually need to run an errand," Graham chimed in.

Both brothers turned to look his way. Brooks smirked. "Really? What's her name?"

Graham busied himself putting the remote away and taking his glass back to the bar, which was just off the theater room. His brothers followed him. No way were they going to leave him alone.

Empty glass in hand, he whirled around. "It's just work. Relax. I'm in the middle of a big case. That's all I can say."

They both stared at him, clearly not believing the lie. With a shrug, he turned to the bar and started stacking the glasses and returning the bottles to the shelves on the wall.

"I'm out," Carson said on a sigh. "I'd rather be home with Georgia than try to figure out what Graham is being so cryptic about."

Fine by him. One down. One to go.

From the corner of his eye, Graham saw Brooks eyeing him, arms crossed over his chest. The sound of Carson headed down the hall, the sound of his footsteps growing softer before eventually disappearing. Now that Carson was gone, Graham waited for the accusations from his twin.

"Whatever you're smirking about, get it off your chest," Graham finally said, turning to face Brooks.

With a shrug, he replied, "Nothing in particular.

Just curious as to why you're rushing off. I'm sure you could do anything work related from here. I know you have your laptop at the ready at all times. And I'm sure you know whatever case you're working on like the back of your hand without having to look at any files."

Graham hadn't gotten to the top at such a young age by depending on anyone else. Every case, every file, every opponent in the courtroom was filed away in his mind. He knew every detail backward and forward. He studied his rivals and found their weaknesses so he could annihilate them when they came face-to-face. So Brooks was right, but no way was Graham going to admit such a thing.

"You don't have to know every detail of my personal life," Graham fired back. Okay, maybe that was harsh, but right now, he wanted to get to Eve. "Are we done here?"

Brooks blew out a sigh. "For now. I'll let you have your little secret, but all secrets come out eventually. Just ask Sutton."

The jab hit too close to home. Yes, Sutton's secret baby, aka Carson, had taken nearly three decades to come to the surface. Graham highly doubted Eve's secret would last three months. Soon both families would know that the Winchesters and the Newports were going to be bound together for life.

That thought had Graham reevaluating everything. Eve had every right not to put his name on the birth certificate. She had every right to fight him for custody. She'd lose, but that wasn't the point. The point was, he refused to let his child come into this world in the midst of a feud.

So now Graham had to show her who he really was. Eve had to see him as a compassionate, loving man who would do anything for his child. She had to see that working together was the best thing for all of them. Because he refused to allow any other man to come in and take away this little family. Love didn't have to be a factor. Graham held the power here, and he would get Eve to marry him, ensuring their child carried the Newport name. A marriage based on sexual chemistry was more than enough for him to rethink saying his "I dos."

And that was why Graham was even more eager to get to her house. Soon Eve would see just how perfect they were together.

Eight

Seven o'clock. Most nights she'd still be at the office, but it was Saturday so Eve had opted to come home. She really needed to cut out the weekends for a while. She was exhausted, and her doctor had told her to listen to her body. Well, she was listening and her body was telling her she needed to get rid of these heels and kill the suit. Yoga pants and a tee sounded pretty good right now. Oh, and a ponytail.

She rarely was off her game. Even at home she was always professional because she often did video meetings and had to look the part. Sure, the other day she had on yoga pants and bunny slippers beneath her desk, but she'd put on makeup, earrings and a suit jacket. Boom. She so owned this corporate world.

She'd nearly cried with relief after she washed her face and pulled her hair back. Now that she was comfortable, she had a little boost of energy…and an extremely empty stomach. She'd had an early lunch to work around meetings, but she seriously needed to keep some snacks in her office at work. Her assistant would've gladly gone and gotten her anything, but Eve had her assistant doing so much lately with the acquisition of the Australian company, Eve hated to even ask for a pack of crackers.

Maybe she'd lie in bed, gorge on food and watch a movie on Netflix. A date with herself? Sounded heavenly and completely relaxing. Just what the doctor ordered.

When someone knocked at the back door, Eve nearly cried. Only one person came and went via the French doors overlooking the outdoor living area. The door was conveniently located by the garage Graham used.

She peered down at her attire and shrugged. He'd seen her in her suits, in a ball gown and in her birthday suit, but he'd never seen her in sloppy, I-want-to-be-left-alone mode.

Circling the kitchen island and bypassing the breakfast nook, she reached the French doors. Only the soft glow from the motion lights illuminated Graham's broad frame, slashing a streak of light across one side of his face. His eyes pierced her straight through the glass. There was an intensity to this man that her body couldn't deny. She hated how, even now, especially now, she didn't want to deny him anything. But if she didn't watch out, she would end up hurt. Right now, she had to focus on her baby.

Flicking the lock, she opened one of the doors. Because she knew he wasn't just here for a quick visit, she stepped aside and let him in.

The second Graham was inside, she clicked the lock back into place. When she turned, his eyes raked her, as they always did. She shivered, but was too tired to even appreciate her instant arousal. There had to be some sort of stop button where this physical relationship was concerned. Shouldn't they focus on how to make this parenting thing work? The time for selfish desires and needs had come to an end.

"If you're here for—"

He held up a hand. "I'm not."

When he took a step forward, closing the gap between them, Eve waited for his familiar touch. But he simply held her gaze and offered a gentle smile. "I'm here for strictly innocent reasons."

Eve laughed, waiting for him to deliver the rest of the punch line. When he only quirked a brow, she sobered. "Innocent? Honey, you don't have an innocent bone in your body."

Honey? Had she seriously just used that term? Exhaustion had obviously stolen her common sense.

"I don't mean to be rude, but really. Why are you here?"

Graham took her elbow and guided her through the house. Her house. As if he owned the place. And she was allowing this to happen. Then he led her up the stairs, toward her bedroom, and pulled back the pristine white duvet on her king-size four-poster bed. Eve darted her eyes between the inviting bed and the confusing man.

"Okay, what's going on?"

Graham took her hand and ushered her into bed. "I had no plans until I got here. But now that I see you're practically swaying on your feet, we're going to relax."

"We?" Eve slid into bed because the temptation was far too great for her to fight.

"That's right." Graham picked up the remote, hit a few buttons. The flat screen slid up from the entertainment island that separated the bed from the sitting area. "I'm going to watch a classic with you."

Okay. So if she had all of this straight in her head, Graham had just appeared at her back door not looking for sex, but to watch a movie and…snuggle?

Eve continued to stare as Graham as climbed into bed beside her and began studying her remote. After several minutes of muttering under his breath—something about his law degree being useless—he finally figured it out. Instantly the room filled with music as the movie popped up, and Eve had to brace herself. He was legitimately here to watch a movie. They were in her bed…completely clothed.

"You're still staring and you're going to miss this opening," Graham said without looking her way.

Her gaze went to the large screen and she instantly recognized *An Affair to Remember*. It was one of her favorite movies. But how did he know? They'd certainly never discussed such personal things.

"Why are you doing this?"

Graham sighed, paused the movie and glanced her way. Those striking blue eyes pierced her heart. But she couldn't have her heart involved, not with him, not now. Her emotions were simply all over the place. She couldn't act on any temporary feelings.

"I love old movies. I want to do absolutely nothing right now but watch one with you. We both work too hard, and now we're having a baby. Maybe it's time we get to know each other."

Without another word, he took the movie off pause, turned the volume up and reached for her hand. The detail-oriented nerd in her wanted to know what was going on. Was this a date? Albeit a warped version of one. Was this some ploy to get her to fall for him? If so, he was doing a damn good job. Did he truly want to get to know her?

Eve attempted to concentrate on the movie, but between exhaustion and the way Graham's thumb drew lazy patterns over the back of her hand, she was having a difficult time.

What was Graham up to? The man was ruthless in a courtroom, if his reputation around Chicago was any indicator. He could've easily had her undressed and beneath him had he tried, because denying him was nearly impossible. Yet he seemed all too happy to lie here, hold her hand and do absolutely nothing.

Graham Newport was playing some sort of game and if she didn't figure out the rules soon, she was going to find herself on the losing side. And that was not an option because she'd end up hurt. Eve had been dealt enough by the hand of grief to last a lifetime and she wasn't looking for more.

Graham knew she'd fallen asleep within the first ten minutes of the movie. Her hand had gone lax beneath his and she even began to snore quietly. He found himself watching her and smiling. Okay, this little plan of his had backfired in a major way.

He'd come here for one reason—to start his plan of seduction. Getting her to trust him, to maybe even develop stronger feelings for him, was a must for making sure they came to a mutual understanding where their child was concerned. And when he asked her to be his wife, he was determined that she'd say yes.

Graham refused to get into a tug-of-war with her over the baby. He refused to allow his child to be a pawn in any family feud, let alone between him and Eve.

But the second she'd opened the door and let him in, he'd seen just how tired she was. She was struggling to keep her eyes open. Was she not sleeping well at night? Was she not feeling well because of morning sickness? Was she working too hard?

Knowing Eve, she'd put 110 percent into her day as usual and then dragged herself home to rest in private. He knew she was trying to figure out what he was doing here, why he'd shown up and hadn't stripped her and made love to her right away. Every part of him wanted nothing more than to peel her out of her T-shirt and leggings. She'd looked damn good dressed down.

And that was a problem. Seeing Eve in an evening gown was heart-stopping. The way a killer suit hugged her hips nearly had him begging. But when she was just herself, makeup-free and wearing casual clothes, she was the most dangerous. He wanted to think this side of Eve was only for him, that she didn't expose this part of herself to anyone.

He shouldn't want to get more deeply involved with her, but he was a selfish bastard. He wanted all of her. She was the mother of his child and she was his. He didn't give up on anything he wanted, and he'd never wanted anything more than to be a father.

This realization hit him hard. Never before had he thought about having a child, yet now he could think of little else. He may not have had a father figure growing up, but he knew the love of a parent. He knew how to put his own needs aside to care for a child and make sure they had a secure life.

The movie had ended, and the room got dark. Graham turned off the TV, sliding the screen back into the island. Silence filled the room, save for Eve's soft snores. Pale light from the hall lamp gave enough of a glow for him to see. Graham reached across the bed and smoothed the silken strands of hair from her face. Instantly Eve startled awake. Her heavy-lidded eyes locked onto his.

"Sorry," he murmured. "I didn't mean to wake you."

Eve blinked and sat straight up against her mound of pillows. "I never make it through a movie on a good day, let alone when I'm already tired."

"Are you not sleeping well?" Concern had him scooting a bit closer. There was too much space between them, literally and figuratively.

"I'm sleeping fine. That's the problem. I want to sleep all the time. The doctor said that was normal in the first trimester."

A wave of relief washed over him. He knew absolutely nothing about pregnancies, so hearing any morsel of doctor's advice was comforting. He needed to start reading anything and everything he could get his hands on about this. He wanted to be able to connect with her, to comfort her, and somehow show her that he was there and she wouldn't be doing this alone.

"Maybe you should cut back a bit each day at work until this trimester passes." Her bored glare was all the answer he needed. Not that he thought she'd readily agree, but still. "You've only got a few more weeks. Then, when you're feeling better, you can add those hours back on."

"Can I?" she asked, her tone mocking. "I'm so glad to have your permission."

Raking a hand through his hair, Graham came to his feet and rounded the bed. "That's not what I meant and you know it. I'm worried about you."

"About the baby," she corrected.

"Fine. I'm worried for both of you." And he was. Only a total jerk would ignore the mother's needs. "I want what's best for both of you."

Eve stared up at him. A red crease mark from her pillow marred the right side of her cheek, but her eyes were actually refreshed. Her ponytail had slid to one side of her head, random strands had escaped and hung down one side. Yeah, he knew nobody got this view of her, and part of him puffed up with conceit that he was the one here with her.

"I can't do this with you."

Confused, Graham lost focus on her sexy, disheveled look. "Excuse me?"

She waved a hand in the air. "This...whatever this is. Your attempt to get to know me or vie for some affection. I don't know what you're doing, but I'm not playing games now, Graham. We're having a baby—that doesn't mean we have to be a couple."

Why did those words feel like a slice to his... what? Heart? His heart wasn't supposed to be involved. But he sure as hell didn't like that she was so quick to put him on the back burner. That wouldn't work with his plan, not one bit. But he wasn't about to give up. He'd barely gotten started.

"Maybe I want to make sure we stay on the same track," he retorted. "Perhaps I want to stay friends with the mother of my baby so we can make this child's life as amazing as possible without turmoil."

"Are we friends?" she asked. "Seriously. We have amazing sex and we're both workaholics. That's about all we have in common. Can a friendship be built on that?"

Graham shrugged. "I've had friendships built on less."

Eve seemed to study him for a moment before her eyes darted down to her lap where she toyed with the hem of her oversize tee. "It's getting late," she whispered.

If she thought he'd take that as a cue to leave, she didn't know him. Obviously that was the entire point of his being here. Why did this seem so forced? Why had everything seemed so easy up until very recently?

Because sex was easy. It was all the emotions that made the struggle real.

"Do you want me to go?" he asked, needing to hear her say it, but refusing to beg for anything. He eased a hip onto the bed next to her. "Do you want me to leave you alone and simply wait for texts about our child? Because you have to know that's not my style. I'm not a man who waits for anything. When I want something, I take it."

Her mesmerizing eyes slowly came up to his. "And what is it you want? The baby, I know. But we're a package, Graham. Don't you see that? I don't even know how we're going to make this work. You and I aren't together, our families hate each other and your brother is so angry and hurt, he's ready to destroy my father given any opportunity."

Tears welled up in her eyes and the sight was something Graham wished he never had to see. "Right now, all that matters is this child. Not your father, not my brother and not this fight. I don't want you worrying about this, Eve. It's not good for the baby."

She burst into tears. Full-on, hands-over-her-face sobbing. What had he said? Obviously the wrong thing when he was only trying to help. No wonder men and women never seemed to be on the same page. They weren't even in the same book.

Clearly words were getting him nowhere and he wasn't about to leave when she was so upset. Wrapping an arm around her, he pulled her against his chest as she continued to cry. Stroking her back, he attempted some comforting words, but he doubted she could hear them.

Moments passed and Graham had to wonder if there was something else that was upsetting her. Surely this wasn't just him. But with all the weight of everything coming down on her, she was bound to break. He didn't want her broken, but if she had to lean on someone, he wanted it to be him. No other man would be coming in here, not when she was carrying his child.

Eve wasn't weak, she wasn't vulnerable, yet right now she was having a moment. He wouldn't embarrass her by asking what he could do. She wouldn't want anyone coming to her rescue. He may not know much about her, but he recognized pride. Actions always trumped words anyway, so he'd show her how he cared instead of just talking about it.

Finally, Eve eased away, wiping at her damp cheeks with the back of her hands.

"Don't say you're sorry," he interjected when she opened her mouth.

"I'm not." She offered a soft smile. "You should've left me to have my meltdown. I can't believe you stayed."

"What kind of jerk do you think I am? I'm not just going to leave."

Closing her eyes, she blew out a breath. "I don't know what to think right now or what your angle is, but I don't think you're a jerk."

His angle? Simple. He wanted his child to be raised with the Newport name. He wanted her to willingly give him rights, and if he had to marry her to get them, then he would. Being around Eve was no hardship and his ache for her hadn't diminished in the slightest.

Before he could comment, her stomach growled. Graham laughed. "Hungry?"

She wrapped her arms around her waist as if to

ward off any other sounds. "Actually, I was going to get something when you knocked. Then you guided me up here and the bed was so inviting. I haven't eaten since early lunch."

Graham came to his feet. "Stay here. I'll get something."

Eve rolled her eyes. "I'm not bedridden. I can make myself something to eat."

"I'm sure you can, but I'm here." Graham stepped back when Eve swung her legs over the side of the bed. "Stubborn, aren't you?"

Even with her red-rimmed eyes and pink-tipped nose, her smile was like a kick to his chest.

"A trait we both possess. Sounds like we'll have a strong-willed child."

Graham smiled. The idea of his child being strong, independent and a go-getter was absolutely perfect. A healthy combination of mother and father...he'd never given it much thought, but their child would be a perfect Newport.

Eve got to her feet and attempted to readjust her hair. Finally, she jerked the ponytail holder out and gathered up the fallen strands. In a flash, she had the mass of hair piled back atop her head.

"You don't have to stay," she told him. "I'm just going to make a quick sandwich and go to bed."

"You're trying so hard to get me out of here." He tipped her chin up and stepped in closer, so close the heat from her body warmed him. "I'm going to make sure you eat and then I'm going to make sure you're all settled in. We'll make small talk—we may even share a laugh. We can talk about the weather or we can talk about the baby. Up to you. But I'm not leaving, Eve. I'm going to be here, so you better get used to it."

"Is that a threat?" she asked with a soft smile.

He kissed her, hard, fast, then released her. "It's a promise."

Nine

Eve rolled over in bed, glanced at the clock and closed her eyes again.

Wait. She jerked up in bed and stared at the glaring numbers. How did it get to be so late? Sleeping in had never been an issue for her. She always showed up before anyone else and got a jump start on her day. At this rate, she was never going to make it into the office on time.

The sudden jolt of movement had her morning sickness hitting her fast. She rushed to the en suite bathroom and fell to her knees.

She'd had worse mornings, but still, she didn't like this feeling one bit. How could she remain professional if she was showing up late and looking like death?

Once she was done, she wiped her face with a cool, damp cloth and realized two things: one, it was Sunday so she wasn't late for anything. And two, there was a glorious smell coming from the kitchen and overtaking her home.

Surprisingly, whatever that scent was, it didn't make her more nauseous. If anything, her stomach was ready to go. This roller coaster of emotions and cravings was extremely difficult to keep up with.

Eve thought back to last night when Graham had made a simple grilled cheese sandwich and cut up an apple for her. Then he'd practically patted her on the head and sent her to bed, saying he'd lock up.

So, either he'd stayed and that was him in the kitchen, or one of her sisters was here. She highly doubted Nora or Grace had come by just to do some cooking, so she had to assume Graham had made himself at home.

Considering that she'd just tossed her cookies, so to speak, she opted to brush her teeth before heading down. By the time she hit the bottom steps, her mouth was watering. The magnificent aroma filled the entire first floor. Suddenly her belly growled and she had no idea how she could go from sick one second to hungry the next. Pregnancy sure wasn't predictable.

Heading down the wide hall toward the back of the house and the kitchen, Eve tried to figure out what to say to Graham. She'd seriously had a meltdown last night. He'd been so concerned about the baby, about her. But she hadn't been able to control those insane emotions.

Years ago when she'd thought herself in love, she'd have given anything for her boyfriend to have cared about her, about their baby. But she'd endured the first trimester and part of the second alone. Then she'd struggled through the miscarriage, the D & C, the grieving. All of it on her own. She'd pushed her sisters away because nobody could fix her broken heart. Nobody could bring back her baby and she wanted to be left alone.

Graham was most likely worried about his place in their child's life. He wasn't the type of man to sit back and let someone else raise his child. Still, the fact he'd stayed last night showed the type of man he was. He could've walked away.

So what did this mean? Did he want more than just shared parenting? Did he want to try at a relationship?

Good morning, shoulders.

Freezing midstride, Eve stared straight ahead to the sexiest cook she'd ever seen. She'd seen Graham countless times with nothing on, but finding him in just his jeans standing at her stove was like some sort of domestic porn. Seriously. This was calendar material. Forget the firefighters, sign Graham up. The way those back muscles flexed and relaxed as he did…whatever it was he was doing.

There was a man cooking in her house. The sexy, hot father of her baby was cooking in her house.

This sight alone was enough to make her want to strip and see if they could make use of that kitchen island, but she'd promised herself no more. She needed to focus on so many other things and her sex life was going to have to take a backseat for a while. What a shame, when she was facing such a delectable sight.

"You're just in time."

He didn't turn around as he spoke, just continued to bustle about getting breakfast ready as if this were the most normal thing in the world. As if he belonged here.

Eve couldn't move from the doorway. Between last night and this morning, she had no clue what Graham had planned next. Not one time did he try to get her undressed. Maybe he didn't find her as appealing as he used to. Perhaps pregnant women were a turnoff. Granted, it wasn't like she felt sexy at the moment.

No matter, she wasn't looking for more. At this point, her only hope was that she could keep the peace in her family when they found out she was carrying a Newport's baby.

"Why did you stay?"

Graham froze, plates in hand. Throwing a glance over his shoulder, he held her with his intense stare. "Because someone needs to make sure you're taking care of yourself."

"So you're my keeper now? I'm old enough to take care of myself."

She didn't mention the fact that he was younger than her. There was no need to state the obvious. But the fact that he'd stayed out of pity didn't sit well with her. Maybe she'd gotten her hopes up too high to think he'd stayed simply because he cared.

"I'm not saying you can't." He dished up some type of casserole and…was that fried apples? "It's the weekend. I wanted to stay and make you breakfast, so I did."

She wanted to argue, but the second she took a seat at the island and he placed that plate in front of her, she had no idea what they'd been on the verge of bickering about.

Eve stared down at her plate of food, which looked like it came from some cooking magazine—not the kind featuring light cuisine, either. Then she glanced at Graham, who was scooping up his own servings.

"You cook?" Okay, that was a stupid question. Clearly elves weren't involved. "I mean, this is more than just oatmeal or cereal for breakfast. Where did you learn this?"

Graham set his plate down and went back for two large glasses of orange juice. After putting everything on the island, he took a seat on a stool next to her.

"My grandma Gerty taught us all about cooking.

It may have seemed like punishment at the time, but looking back I can see she did it out of love, and as a way to bond."

The wistfulness layered with the love in his tone told her this grandmother was one special lady. Eve pierced one gooey apple with her fork. The buttery, cinnamon sugar flavors exploded in her mouth. She prayed this food stayed with her. This was definitely too good to waste.

"Tell me about Gerty," Eve said, forking up a bite of some egg, sausage and cheese casserole. "Is she still alive?"

Graham swallowed and shook his head. "No."

That one word, full of sadness, had Eve pausing with her fork midway to her mouth. "Oh. Um… sorry. I didn't think."

Graham barely spared glance look her way. "No reason for you to be sorry. She passed away several years back. But she was like a second mother to us. Mom met Gerty at a coffee shop. Gerty was retiring, but she'd already taken a liking to Mom. The two were close and Mom moved in with Gerty because she needed help."

A single, pregnant woman. Eve's fork clattered to her plate as she thought of the parallel between Graham's mother's situation and hers. Did he see it? Is that why he was so adamant about helping her? Did he want to make up for the sins of some faceless man? Graham was so loyal, so noble where his family was concerned.

"Don't go there."

Eve jerked her gaze to Graham, who had shifted on his stool to face her.

"Don't let your mind betray you," he added. "I'm not pitying you because of my mother's circumstances. I'm sure she was scared being single and pregnant, but that's not why I'm here."

Resting her palms on the edge of the counter, Eve tipped her head. "Why are you here? What do you want, Graham? Just say it."

His aqua eyes sparkled, and his lips pursed just slightly, reminding her of what she'd been missing out on the past few days. "Maybe I want to get to know you more. Maybe I think you need to know me better, as well. We need to be strong together, for the sake of our baby and our families."

Eve couldn't agree more, but the way he looked at her said he wanted more than just pleasantries. Could she deny him? Probably not, but she did wholeheartedly agree with him that they needed to work together.

"Then you'll have to stop eye-flirting with me," she told him, resuming her amazing breakfast.

"Eye-flirting?"

"Yes." She stabbed another apple with her fork. "You look at me and I can see you undressing me in your mind, but you haven't made any attempt to do so. I can't figure you out, but I can't be on the receiving end of that stare anymore."

Eve froze midchew as Graham's fingertip slid

along her jawbone. Quickly, she finished her bite so she didn't choke. Her body responded instantly and he'd barely touched her. Why did she have to still want him? Why couldn't she get him out of her system?

"I'll strip you right now and take you on this counter." He turned her head toward him, his eyes darting to her mouth. "Say the word."

Oh, she wanted to say the word. Any word. Anything that would turn this passion into action. But she had to think straight…didn't she? She'd told herself not to fall back into the pattern of sleeping with him. That would be all too easy…and all too amazingly delicious.

No. She couldn't. They couldn't work as a team to figure out how to deal with the pregnancy and their families if their clothes were always falling off.

"Oh, my word, that wind is…"

Eve and Graham jerked their attention to the back door where Nora stood, her hair blown around her face, her mouth wide, her eyes even wider. There was a toss-up as to who was more shocked.

"You've got to be kidding me," Nora finally stated, shaking her long hair away from her face.

There was no reason to deny anything. Seriously. What could Eve say? Graham was sitting right here, shirtless, and Eve had clearly just crawled out of bed. Denying anything at this point would only make Eve look like a fool and insult her sister's intelligence.

"Plenty of breakfast if you want some," Graham

YOUR PARTICIPATION IS REQUESTED!

Dear Reader,

Since you are a lover of our books – we would like to get to know you!

Inside you will find a short Reader's Survey. Sharing your answers with us will help our editorial staff understand who you are and what activities you enjoy.

To thank you for your participation, we would like to send you 2 books and 2 gifts – **ABSOLUTELY FREE!**

Enjoy your gifts with our appreciation,

Pam Powers

SEE INSIDE FOR READER'S SURVEY

For Your Reading Pleasure...

We'll send you 2 books and 2 gifts
ABSOLUTELY FREE
just for completing our Reader's Survey!

YOURS FREE!
We'll send you two fabulous surprise gifts absolutely FREE, just for trying our books!

YOUR READER'S SURVEY
"THANK YOU" FREE GIFTS INCLUDE:
- ▶ 2 FREE books
- ▶ 2 lovely surprise gifts

PLEASE FILL IN THE CIRCLES COMPLETELY TO RESPOND

1) What type of fiction books do you enjoy reading? (Check all that apply)
- ○ Suspense/Thrillers ○ Action/Adventure ○ Modern-day Romances
- ○ Historical Romance ○ Humor ○ Paranormal Romance

2) What attracted you most to the last fiction book you purchased on impulse?
- ○ The Title ○ The Cover ○ The Author ○ The Story

3) What is usually the greatest influencer when you <u>plan</u> to buy a book?
- ○ Advertising ○ Referral ○ Book Review

4) How often do you access the internet?
- ○ Daily ○ Weekly ○ Monthly ○ Rarely or never.

5) How many NEW paperback fiction novels have you purchased in the past 3 months?
- ○ 0 - 2 ○ 3 - 6 ○ 7 or more

YES! I have completed the Reader's Survey. Please send me the 2 FREE books and 2 FREE gifts (gifts are worth about $10) for which I qualify. I understand that I am under no obligation to purchase any books, as explained on the back of this card.

225/326 HDL GKET

FIRST NAME	LAST NAME

ADDRESS

APT.#	CITY

STATE/PROV.	ZIP/POSTAL CODE

READER SERVICE—Here's how it works:

Accepting your 2 free Harlequin Desire® books and 2 free gifts (gifts valued at approximately $10.00) places you under no obligation to buy anything. You may keep the books and gifts and return the shipping statement marked "cancel." If you do not cancel, about a month later we'll send you 6 additional books and bill you just $4.55 each in the U.S. or $5.24 each in Canada. That is a savings of at least 13% off the cover price. It's quite a bargain! Shipping and handling is just 50¢ per book in the U.S. and 75¢ per book in Canada.* You may cancel at any time, but if you choose to continue, every month we'll send you 6 more books, which you may either purchase at the discount price or return to us and cancel your subscription. *Terms and prices subject to change without notice. Prices do not include applicable taxes. Sales tax applicable in N.Y. Canadian residents will be charged applicable taxes. Offer not valid in Quebec. Books received may not be as shown. All orders subject to approval. Credit or debit balances in a customer's account(s) may be offset by any other outstanding balance owed by or to the customer. Please allow 4 to 6 weeks for delivery. Offer available while quantities last.

supplied with that darn sexy grin. Clearly he was going the hospitable route instead of the awkward one.

Eve couldn't help the laugh that escaped her.

Nora's eyes narrowed on Graham before she turned to Eve. "You think this is funny? I thought you two were done...whatever it was you were doing."

Eve started to stand, but Graham put a hand on her arm. "We're not done, as a matter of fact."

Eve cringed. If he said anything about the baby, there would be nothing to stop Nora from telling Grace. Eve really needed to be the one to tell her sisters...and not in front of Graham. This was definitely a private matter she needed to handle on her own.

"Eve, come on." Nora stepped into the kitchen, her eyes locked on Eve's. "They're trying to destroy Dad's name, his reputation. You of all people should get how damning that could be, not only to our family, but to the company. They think he's hiding secrets, but he's a dying man. Why would he keep secrets at this point?"

Nora had just wrapped up and delivered the crux of the entire situation in that one question. Why indeed? That the matter was out of her control made this whole pregnancy even scarier. There had to be a way to keep this baby safe from family backlash.

"You're not telling me anything I don't already know," Eve replied, purposely keeping her voice calm, though her heart was pounding hard in her chest. "Graham and I are keeping everything private." For now. "So this doesn't need to go any further." Also, for now. "Did you need something from me?"

Nora blinked, then shook her head. "Seriously? You're going to brush this off?"

"There's nothing to brush off," Eve corrected. Now she did slide out from beneath Graham's touch so she could stand and approach her sister. "What Graham and I are doing, or not doing, is really only our business."

Was she honestly going to put Graham above her sisters' feelings right now? Eve was dangerously close to relationship territory, to an area neither of them ever wanted to be. But he'd stood firm against Brooks regarding the media backlash; that much was obvious from the pullback in the coverage. Perhaps they had already crossed that line and that was something she'd have to think about later.

"Eve wasn't feeling well last night, so I stayed to make sure she was okay," Graham chimed in. "Then I made breakfast and was going to head home after we ate. Now that I know she's feeling better, I'm comfortable leaving."

The weight on her chest vanished as she realized he wasn't about to share their secret.

Nora gave him a suspicious look. "You mean you stayed and took care of her because...why? You care about her? Eve, come on. You have to see he's using you. He's using you to get closer to Dad."

The accusation hurt. She knew for a fact Graham wasn't using her. He wasn't. He wouldn't take what they shared and turn it against her. Just because he hated her father didn't mean he'd be so cruel to her. And she hated that her sister didn't think someone like Graham would want to be with Eve simply because he found her attractive.

"I'm not using her. In fact, I asked Brooks to retract the media statements he made regarding your father."

Nora's eyes narrowed once again. Eve couldn't blame her sister for being so skeptical. Eve would feel the same way if the roles were reversed. Nora wouldn't understand there was much more to Eve and Graham than met the eye. And Nora wouldn't understand because Eve didn't fully understand it herself.

Another wave of nausea swept over her and Eve swayed on her feet. She gripped the stool and closed her eyes. Instantly Graham had his strong hands around her waist.

"Eve? What?"

She squeezed her eyes tighter, willing the unwanted nausea away. She couldn't answer for fear of getting sick right here. She hoped staying still for just a moment would help…

"Eve, talk to me," Graham urged. "Is it the baby?"

"Baby?" Nora exclaimed.

Suddenly Eve's fear of getting sick wasn't the issue. Now her sister knew and there was nothing Eve could do to stop this train wreck.

Ten

Graham didn't give a damn about the slipup. And he could care even less if Nora was shocked. When Eve swayed and caught herself on the barstool, his protective instincts took over.

Scooping her up in his arms, Graham ignored her weak plea to put her down as he carted her over to the living area off the kitchen. Once he laid her on the sofa, he noticed her pallor and the sheen of sweat that dotted her forehead. He eased himself onto the sofa beside her and lifted her legs onto his lap.

"Get her a cold cloth," he ordered Nora without taking his eyes from Eve. What if something was wrong? Why did she look so damn pale?

Eve laid one hand on her stomach and the other over her forehead. "I'm fine. Just give me a minute."

Seconds later, Nora waved a washcloth in Graham's face. He used it to wipe Eve's forehead, her neck. He didn't like this helpless feeling one bit. He'd seen his grandmother and his mother grow weak and pass. Not that Eve was dying, but the thought that there was nothing he could do for her right now really pissed him off.

"Eve." Nora stood over the back of the couch and reached down to smooth a damp strand of hair from her sister's face. "Are you pregnant again?"

Eve groaned, muttering something Graham didn't comprehend because he'd homed in on the key word in Nora's question.

Again?

What the hell did Nora mean by that? When had Eve been pregnant before?

"I'm pregnant," Eve mumbled. "Don't tell Grace. I'll tell her."

"Oh, honey." Now Nora's voice took on a compassionate tone, one that Graham instinctively knew had everything to do with this former pregnancy. He was almost afraid to find out the details, but he would. "How far along are you?"

"Seven weeks now."

Graham listened to the sisters, but his mind was overloaded. A spear of unexpected jealousy hit him square in the chest. He had no right to be jealous of a faceless man who'd created a baby with Eve. Clearly they weren't together anymore. But still, Graham didn't want to think of her experiencing this with anyone else.

"Promise me," Eve was saying, her eyes pleading with Nora. "Don't say anything. Let Graham and me handle this. We want what's best for the baby, and our families have to come to some sort of peace."

Nora glanced at Graham before looking back down at Eve. "I promise. I know what it's like to be pregnant and unsure of what to do next."

Nora had been a single mother before she and Reid had fallen in love. Graham didn't know much about Nora's circumstances, but it sounded as though she'd been alone and scared. Fortunately, Eve wouldn't be alone. Ever, if he had any say.

Eve started to sit up, waving her hand when Graham tried to ease her back down. "It passed. I'm fine. I'm just going to sit here for a bit." Looking over her shoulder, she asked, "What did you need this morning, Nora?"

"What? Oh, it's not important." Nora smiled, then wrapped her arms around her sister. "I thought we might go shopping for party costumes for Halloween, but we can go another day."

Again, Graham didn't like being left out of this little shopping trip. Didn't like being so easily dismissed as though he was replaceable.

"I'll feel fine in the afternoon if you want to wait."

Nora stood straight up and nodded. "Sounds good. Text me later. Reid doesn't want to go, so I'll just pick something up for him. But I was given a list of things he refuses to wear. Tights being at the top of the list."

"No Robin Hood for him, then." Eve smiled. "Thanks for understanding and keeping this to yourself. I know you have questions, but I'll address them. Just not now."

Graham watched the younger Winchester sister as she adjusted her cardigan and smoothed her hair back. "I promise to keep this all to myself, but if you need any help with doctor's appointments or someone to—"

"She's got someone," Graham stated. "Just be sure to keep that promise."

Nora pulled in a breath as if she wanted to let him have it, but Graham flashed her what he hoped was a charming smile. No way in hell was he letting anyone else care for Eve and his child. They may not be a couple, but she belonged to him now.

Closing her mouth without saying anything, Nora turned on her heel and left out the front door. Silence filled the spacious room. Eve's legs were still in Graham's lap, but she sat up with her arm stretched across the back of the sofa.

"We're going to have to tell your brothers now," she said, rubbing her head. "I'll have to talk to Grace and…this is just going to be a mess."

"This isn't a mess. If our families can't see that a child is more important than our rivalry, then—"

"Tell me more about Gerty." Eve's eyes held his. She reached down and took his hand.

"Excuse me?"

Eve glanced down, traced a pattern over his palm. "You seemed so happy when you were talking about her. You seemed nostalgic and that's a side of you I don't know."

Graham swallowed. She didn't know this side because it was the one that was most vulnerable. But he wanted her to fully know him, to gain her affection so that his plan would be flawless. In order for that to happen, he'd have to bare all his emotions where his past was concerned.

"Gerty was amazing." Because he couldn't sit still, he shifted from beneath her and went to the kitchen for her plate. After putting it on her lap, he set her juice on the side table. "She'd swat our hands with a wooden spoon if we cursed, then just as lovingly show us how to bake homemade bread. I've never known anyone like her."

Eve continued to hold on to her plate. Graham picked up the fork and got a small bite for her. When he lifted it to her lips, she kept her gaze on his as he fed her.

"When I fell off the monkey bars in the first grade, she came right to the school because she didn't want to worry my mom or disrupt her shift at the coffee shop. By the time Mom got home, Gerty had bandaged me up, given me ice cream for dinner, and we were watching *Casablanca*."

Eve smiled as he lifted another bite to her mouth. "You get your love of old movies from her."

Graham nodded. "I get many things from her. She would always say how she was just a waitress, but she took pride in her job. She told us to do whatever job we wanted, whether it be a janitor or a doctor. She wanted us to know that every job was important and to make sure we worked hard."

Graham recalled her harping on how important hard work was time and time again. No matter the career, they had to put 110 percent into it. She was a proud woman and Graham knew his mother had found a real-life angel just when she'd needed her. Or perhaps they'd needed each other, considering that Gerty's husband had just passed when she took in Cynthia.

Graham continued to feed Eve. He shared random stories about his childhood. Whatever popped into his mind, he shared. For once, he was completely relaxed. Surprisingly, he wanted Eve to be fully aware of where he came from. He didn't come from money. He'd worked his ass off to get where he was at the law firm.

After her plate was completely clean, he reached for the juice and handed it to her.

"That was amazing," she told him. "Feel free to cook for me anytime."

Graham stilled. He wasn't prepared to play house. He had no road map, no plan here. All he knew was the end result had to be that his child was raised as a Newport.

"I'm sorry," she told him, glancing away. "I didn't mean that the way it sounded."

"Don't be sorry."

Shaking her head, she put her plate and glass on the table before leaning back on the couch. "You may be able to keep those emotions hidden in the courtroom, but I can read you better than you think. I understand you don't want a relationship with me, or any type of commitment. I wasn't implying that."

Graham raked a hand over his face; the stubble on his jawline was itchy and annoying. "Neither of us is at a point in our lives when we can put forth the time and attention a relationship needs."

Eve nodded. "I agree."

"But that doesn't mean everything that happened before I found out you were pregnant is over. I can't just shut off my desire for you, Eve. If you want to cool it in that area, tell me now. I'll respect your wishes and I'll still do everything in my power to keep you and this baby safe and cared for."

He had to say what she wanted to hear. He couldn't scare her off this early. He couldn't even hint at what his true intentions were.

Eve pushed to her feet and started pacing. She stopped in front of the fireplace and turned her back to him. His eyes focused beyond her, on the photos she had arranged across the mantel. Every silver-framed picture showcased her family. The sisters,

Eve and her mother, a young Eve on her father's shoulders. He didn't want to get into that aspect of her life. Graham couldn't afford to see Sutton as a loving father. Graham didn't give a damn about Sutton, save for the fact that he knew who Brooks and Graham's birth father was. Or he at least knew a name. The old bastard was keeping this information to himself and Graham would do anything to find it out.

But he wouldn't use Eve or his unborn child to get it.

"I don't know what I want," Eve finally said. "This passion clearly isn't going away anytime soon. But I need some space."

When she turned around, Graham had to force himself to remain seated. She didn't need him cutting her off, she needed him to be strong for her. But he wouldn't stay away long.

"Wanting you has never been a question," she went on. "But—"

"I know." And he did. Graham came to his feet, pleased when her eyes raked over his bare chest. Let her look, let her continue to want and need just as he did. If she needed him, then that would play right into his hand. "I'll give you space, Eve. But you need to understand, I'm not going away. I won't pressure you or point out that you're looking at me like you want to take the rest of my clothes off."

Eve rolled her eyes. "So arrogant."

"Accurate, not arrogant," he corrected as he

slowly closed the space between them. "I'm going to check on you every day. I'm going to be involved with this pregnancy. But you're going to come to me on your own."

He now stood so close to her that his bare chest rubbed against her T-shirt.

She tipped her head back. "You're sure of that?"

Graham eased closer, his lips within a breath of hers. "Positive."

He brushed his lips against hers, not quite kissing her, but feeling her warm breath. The slight whimper that escaped her was reassuring, but he stepped back. Fisting his hands at his sides to remain in control, he counted backward from ten.

She wanted space? So be it. She'd see just how difficult ignoring this desire would be.

"I'll call you later."

Graham forced himself to walk away. After getting his clothes and letting himself out, he reevaluated the plan in his head. Carson and Brooks needed to know about the baby, but he couldn't tell them just yet. He needed to formulate a better strategy for dealing with the Winchesters that didn't involve obliterating Sutton, and in turn hurting Eve. He didn't want her hurt, he wanted her to be completely and utterly his. But he also wanted Sutton to divulge the name of his father before he died.

Damn it. There had to be a way to get everything he wanted and not hurt Eve in the process.

If Roman could find their birth father soon, Graham knew Brooks would ease off Sutton. Or if Sutton somehow found it in the deepest part of his dark heart to share the information he knew, that would be even better. But Graham feared the man would go to his grave with the secret.

Just like his mother had. Why hadn't she just told them? All Graham had ever heard was how their father wasn't in the picture and she didn't want to talk about him.

So here they were with no answers, other than that Sutton was Carson's father. But that was it.

Putting thoughts of Sutton out of his mind, Graham pulled away from Eve's house, already planning on how to gain her attention, to make her come to him. Because he wouldn't beg for any women…not even the mother of his child.

Eleven

Graham eased back in his chair and thanked God the case he'd been waiting on to go to trial was finally scheduled. This would be a slam dunk for his client, and another win for Graham and the firm.

Since she'd last seen him, he'd randomly texted Eve. He purposely didn't flirt, didn't get into anything sexual or do the whole pathetic what-are-you-wearing thing. Nope. He wanted to keep her guessing, because if she was guessing, then she was thinking about him and his next move. And if she was thinking about him, then her thoughts would travel to the bedroom all on their own.

But the wait was killing him. It had been too long since he'd touched her properly. The thought of having another woman didn't excite him in the least. Eve was the woman he wanted in his bed, or anywhere else he could get her all to himself.

He knew she was getting ready for her sister's upcoming costume party, but he still wanted to see her. She couldn't come to him fast enough.

"Mr. Newport." His assistant's soft voice came through the speaker. "You have a visitor."

Eve? No, that was ridiculous. She wouldn't come here, not after she'd exploded when he'd shown up at her office during business hours.

"Shall I send Carson in?"

Graham came to his feet and pressed the speaker button. "Yes. Thank you."

Graham's door swung open and Carson stepped inside, closing the door at his back.

"You have a minute?"

Graham gestured to the seat across from his desk. "Of course."

"I'll be brief." Carson remained standing, so Graham did, too. "I'm going to see Sutton this evening. He called me yesterday and wanted to meet. I've been hesitant, but his time is limited, so I'm going."

Graham stilled. "Alone?"

"I know you and Brooks want answers from him, so if you want to go, we can all meet there. That bastard thinks he can always get what he wants, but we're a team, so we're in this together."

Another encounter with Sutton? Why not. The more they pumped him for answers, the greater the odds he'd wear down and just tell them what they wanted to know.

"Is Brooks going?"

Carson nodded. "He's meeting me there."

Graham glanced at the files on his desk, the open emails on his computer screen waiting to be answered. Nothing was more important than another shot with Sutton. Their time was running out.

"What time?" he asked, turning back to his brother.

"Seven."

Graham gave a firm nod of his head. "I'll be there."

Carson pulled in a deep breath and shoved his hands in his pockets. "I have no idea what I'm going to say. It's still awkward for me, especially now that he's dying…"

Graham couldn't imagine the emotions Carson was dealing with right now. "Are you sure you don't want to take Georgia instead?"

"No. She understands the need for the three of us to be there. I want to help you guys get the answers you need, plus I want to see what he has to say."

Graham wondered what Eve would say if she knew he was going to see her father. She was protective of him, wouldn't want anyone going to him on his deathbed and pumping him for information. Still, Graham was going to try one last time. Who knew when the man was going to pass? Sutton may have still been getting the best care at his sprawling estate, but that was only because of his billions. He was too proud to be in some facility like everyone else.

Had Eve told her father about the baby? Doubtful, or Sutton would've called Graham to meet with him, as well. Was Eve planning on exposing their secret or was she hoping to avoid telling her dad?

"You okay?"

Graham blinked and focused back on his brother. "Yeah. Fine. I'll finish up here and meet you all over at Sutton's."

Carson let himself out and Graham hurried to finish up the work that needed his attention right now. Once he was done, he grabbed his cell and thought about firing off a text to Eve but opted not to. She didn't need to know what was going on. If Sutton wanted her to know, he could tell her. Graham wasn't putting himself in the middle any more than he already was.

Sutton's affairs were his business, but Sutton's affair with Graham's mom was clearly out in the open now. Considering that Carson wasn't much younger than Graham and Brooks, Graham knew the affair had started when he and Brooks were mere infants. There was no way in hell Sutton wasn't aware of the first name of their father at least. Why did the old bastard care enough to keep it secret? Any information he provided would go a long way to helping them discover who their father was.

But maybe they wouldn't like the answer. Maybe

their father was fully aware of the twins he'd given up. Maybe he didn't want anything to do with them. Still, that was a risk Graham and Brooks were willing to take.

In the end, Graham texted Eve, asking if she'd found a costume for the party. Simple enough, but effective in keeping her on her toes and their lines of communication open.

As soon as he started to shut the lights off in his office, the cell vibrated in his pocket. He pulled it out and nearly sagged against the wall. The image of Eve dressed as some sexy goddess with a white wrap hugging all her tempting curves had him gritting his teeth and cursing himself for telling her he'd give her space. The little vixen was playing games with him. She wanted him begging. He was sure that was her angle.

But two could definitely play at that game and he never played without every intention of winning.

Sutton Winchester's house was a vast estate not too far from the offices where he'd once controlled the real estate world. Graham and Brooks moved in behind Carson as they were led toward the back of the house. The butler was solemn and said nothing as he gestured for them to follow. Not that Graham was expecting a warm welcome, but still.

He tried to take in the surroundings, tried to imagine Eve growing up in this cold mansion. There wasn't a thing out of place and it looked more like a museum than a place where children played.

Graham instantly thought of his penthouse and cringed. Not exactly a playground, but he would make damn sure his child had a fun place to be a kid even if he had to remove his wet bar and put in an indoor jungle gym.

How pathetic was this? He was already one-upping Sutton in his own mind in regards to parenting. Ridiculous.

The servant escorting them motioned toward a set of double doors. Carson thanked the man and threw a glance back at his brothers.

"We've got your back," Brooks stated. "Go in when you're ready."

Carson turned back around, placed his hands on the knobs and eased both doors open. Graham didn't know what he expected, maybe a gray-toned man lying in bed hooked up to machines keeping him alive. But the reality was Sutton sitting up in a plush chair with his feet up by the fire in what Graham assumed was the master suite. A thick, plaid blanket covered his lap.

Sutton was once a kingpin in the corporate world, but right now he looked to be someone's loving grandpa waiting for children to gather around for story time.

Actually, this was his child's grandfather, but Graham would rather forget that little fact and focus on the reason for their visit now.

"I was hoping you'd come alone," Sutton stated. "But I'm not surprised you brought your brothers."

Graham didn't reply. This was Carson's show... for now. Carson had received the invite and it was Carson who had the most to get off his chest. Graham and Brooks were most likely beating the proverbial dead horse. Okay, really poor choice of words, but he couldn't help what popped into his head.

"My brothers and I are a unit. You know all about family loyalty, right?" Carson mocked.

Sutton merely nodded, not answering the rhetorical question.

"I don't even know what to say to you," Carson admitted.

Graham exchanged a knowing look with Brooks. They both knew Carson was on edge, and it definitely cost him to admit it. The poor guy had been on the fence about whether to fully accept Sutton as his father, whether to approach him and listen to what the old man had to say. But they were here now and Graham was more concerned about Carson's feelings than anything else.

"Have a seat." Sutton turned his attention to the twins. "All of you."

Carson remained still, staring at his father. Graham moved first to take a seat on the sofa on the other side of the oriental rug across from Sutton. Brooks sat beside him and finally Carson took the last spot on the end.

Sutton shifted in his seat. Graham wasn't sure if

it was nerves or if the old man was simply trying to get comfortable. Sutton wasn't the type to show his emotions, so Graham doubted he was feeling anything but smug. He'd called Carson to come, and he had.

"Why did you want me here?" Carson finally asked, breaking the silent tension.

"You're my son."

Graham snorted, ignoring Sutton's frown and quick, disapproving look.

"So you're expecting us to get to know each other now that I know the truth and you're sick?" Carson asked.

Sutton turned his face to the fire. Orange flames licked against the black stone. The Chicago air was cooling quite a bit, hinting at an early winter. Graham found it easy to focus on the weather, on the fire, on anything other than the fact he didn't want to be here. Oh, he wanted to be here if he was going to get a name, but the chances of that happening were about as good as Sutton recovering from lung cancer.

"What you decide to do is up to you." Sutton coughed, and that's when it was apparent how sick the man was. This coughing fit wasn't short and it wasn't quiet. Finally, when he was done, he turned back to Carson. "I wanted you to know that I truly loved your mother."

Brooks tensed beside Graham. Of course he'd bring their mother into the conversation. He'd pretend that he knew her well, that he was heartbroken to leave her. Sutton had left Cynthia alone and pregnant, just like he'd found her. Only this time she'd been pregnant with *his* kid and he hadn't known it. Still, a lowly waitress and outsider wouldn't have fit into his high-society world of luxury homes, cars and diamonds.

The atmosphere of anger and bitterness in this room enveloped them all. There was so much to be said, but at the same time they were dealing with a dying man...and Eve's father. The grandfather of Graham's baby.

Graham stared at Sutton and tried to imagine the man from the picture on Eve's mantel. The man who held his daughter on his shoulders at some amusement park. Sutton may be ruthless, he may have had countless affairs, but he loved his children. Considering that he had been shocked by the news of Carson's paternity, Graham wasn't surprised he'd called Carson to his home. Sutton wouldn't sit back and just ignore his child.

But he had no problem ignoring his ex-lover's other children.

"If you loved our mother, then tell us the name of our father," Brooks stated. "You were with her long enough. She would've confided in you."

Sutton shook his head. "It's because I loved Cynthia that I won't betray her confidence. If she'd wanted you to know, she would've told you."

"Tell them." Carson's low demand shocked Graham.

"It's not my place, son."

Carson let out a humorless laugh, eased forward and rested his forearms on his legs. Hands dangling between his knees, he glanced toward Brooks and Graham. Trying to offer silent support, Graham nodded for Carson to go on.

"My brothers deserve to know their father," Carson said, looking back at Sutton. "They keep hitting dead ends. If you can help them—"

"I didn't call them here," Sutton interrupted. "I wanted to see you. I don't have much time, though my doctors keep telling me I'm a fighter. I'm realistic."

"All the more reason for you to tell us," Brooks stated. "You may be the only other person who knows. We don't even know if our birth father is aware of us."

Sutton simply stared back. He gave no hint of what he knew, no sign that he even cared if they were struggling. Graham never liked the man from his dealings with him in the corporate world. He'd been sneaky and underhanded. He kept secrets, even from his staff. Graham had actually seen one of Sutton's previous employees win a case against the old man, but that had been during Graham's internship so he hadn't had a hand in that win.

Graham knew Sutton wasn't about to give up the name, if he even knew a name. For all Graham knew, Sutton was just stringing them along. How had Eve turned out so loyal and honest?

Obviously Eve's mother had a hand in raising her

daughter right and was smart enough to finally leave Sutton after years of unfaithful marriage.

"I want to make something clear," Sutton went on. "Cynthia was the love of my life."

Graham didn't want to hear this, didn't want to be subjected to more lies. But one glance at Carson made Graham realize that his younger brother wanted to know. Not that Carson was naive, but Carson was more prone to forgiveness than Graham or Brooks. So Graham remained silent, though he had plenty of thoughts racing through his mind.

Sutton's eyes didn't leave Carson. "I would've given anything to be with Cynthia. But my wife was so well connected in Chicago society, it would've been career suicide to leave her. Plus, she would've made life hell for Cynthia, and I couldn't allow that."

"Would you have made the same decision if you'd known about me?"

The underlying tone of vulnerability was something Graham had never seen from Carson. Graham's younger brother was a rock, he was always in control, but this little meeting was getting to him. Graham prayed Carson would hold it together.

"I would've gone through hell to be with my son."

Sutton's answer sounded honest. Graham fully believed the man would've sacrificed his marriage to Eve's mother. No doubt Sutton would've wanted a son to raise, to mold into his heir. But Eve had filled that role, and she was doing a remarkable job. Maybe too remarkable.

And just like that, his thoughts had once again strayed to Eve during this meeting. He'd be checking on her again when they left here…especially after that little picture she'd sent to torture him.

"I want to hate you," Carson muttered.

Graham glanced over in time to see Brooks give a manly, reassuring pat to Carson's shoulder. They were here for Carson, to support him. If he wanted to embrace Sutton as his father and live out these days happily ever after, then that's what they'd do. But Graham wasn't so willing to forgive the bastard.

"I know you do," Sutton agreed. "And you have every right. But I couldn't die, not without telling you that Cynthia meant the world to me and I regret not having been there for you."

Graham wasn't surprised that their mother had kept the baby from Sutton. She'd probably been scared of the backlash and it was just as easy to live with Gerty and raise her boys in secret as opposed to facing legal proceedings, which she wouldn't have been able to afford.

Silence filled the room. The fire continued to crackle, sending out wayward flickers and orange sparks. Graham glanced around the room. He thought for sure that he'd see pictures of Eve and her sisters here, but there was nothing. Images of Eve staring at pictures of her father on her computer flashed through Graham's mind. She'd been so eager to get those images uploaded and she'd

scrolled through them as though they were her life-
line to her ailing father.

Graham didn't want Carson to give his loyalty,
his love to Sutton, but this wasn't Graham's choice to
make. Who knew what would happen if and when he
ever found his birth father? Maybe Graham would
find a jerk who knew about his kids and just didn't
care. What then? Would Graham still forgive him or
want to try to make a relationship with him?

"I don't know what to say, honestly." Carson
stared at his hands dangling between his knees. "I'd
like to visit you, maybe see you a little more and
talk. For whatever time we have—"

"I'll take anything," Sutton said, a soft smile
forming on his pale face.

Graham had only seen that smile in Eve's pictures. Apparently he reserved the emotion for his
children. Graham was a bit jealous of how Carson's
journey had ended; he deserved a dad, even if it
was Sutton.

Brooks came to his feet and sighed. "I'm done
here. Carson, stay as long as you like. I'll be outside."

Once Brooks was gone, Graham also stood. He
approached Sutton, knowing this may be the last
time he ever saw the man. He had no intention of
ever coming back.

"I'm glad you're not my father," Graham said,
leaning down just enough so only Sutton could hear.
"But Carson is happy to finally know. If you have

to fake affection, do it. He deserves a father who isn't a jerk."

"I love my son," Sutton said simply.

Graham nodded and straightened. It was so tempting to tell him about the baby. So tempting to get just one final jab in. But Graham wasn't that much of an ass and he'd never do that to Eve. He wanted a chance to show her what a good father he could be and harassing *her* father was not the way to go about that.

Graham turned to his brother. "I'll wait outside with Brooks. Seriously, take your time."

Before Graham had gotten outside, he'd fired off a text to Eve indicating what he'd do to her if he were to ever see her in that Halloween costume.

"That man can rot in hell for all I care." Brooks rested his back against one of the thick, white columns of the portico. "I'm happy for Carson, but damn it. That man is infuriating."

Graham stepped forward, shoving his hands into his pockets and hunching his shoulders against the chilly breeze. "Carson has been on the fence for a while now. He wants to forgive Sutton. I hate to come to the guy's defense, but he didn't know Carson existed."

Brooks jerked his gaze around. "Are you serious? You're going to stand there and make excuses for the guy? If Mom was the love of his life, as he claims, then he would've moved heaven and earth to be with her. And he damn well would give a portion of his estate to his biological son."

When Graham didn't reply, Brooks narrowed his eyes. "This has to do with Eve, doesn't it? You're still hung up on her."

He was the father of her child. Which was a few levels above being "hung up on her."

"I'm stating the obvious, that's all." Graham wasn't about to bring Eve into this discussion. She had enough on her plate without being further caught up in this battle. "Sutton and Carson need time to talk alone. You and I will only make things worse."

Brooks started pacing on the stone walk. "I need Roman to come up with something concrete. I'm putting all my faith in him to find our father."

"I know," Graham said, hating how much this issue was controlling Brooks's life. "But it will happen. We can't run into dead ends forever. Something will turn up. Someone somewhere knows the truth."

Brooks snorted and jerked his thumb toward the house. "Yeah. He's in there."

Graham stared at the double doors. Sutton knew. Absolutely without a doubt he knew. But Graham refused to beg the man. He would find out on his own. He would not give Sutton any satisfaction in getting one up on him. Ever.

Twelve

Seven weeks pregnant and her body was already showing signs of change. Eve attempted to adjust her cleavage in the strips of fabric covering her chest. The white goddess costume had seemed like a good idea at the time, but now she felt very exposed.

Glancing in her floor-length mirror, she shivered as she recalled Graham's text. The man wasn't playing nice. He was trying to get her to give in and… well, she was having a difficult time recalling why she needed to stay away.

Oh, yeah. Someone had to be responsible and think things through right now. Someone had to step back and think straight. When he sent those messages, and there had been many, Eve found it more and more difficult to keep him at a distance.

She hadn't seen him for several days. Too many. The messages hadn't started out as flirty, but then she'd sent that picture and she'd opened up some sort of dam. He'd flooded her phone with messages that would've made her high-society mother blush.

With the cool, windy October weather, Eve would definitely need a coat this evening. Otherwise she'd freeze her butt off.

Eve glanced at the antique clock on her vanity and sighed. She was running late because insecurities over the changes in her body had her doubting her costume. But she had no plan B so goddess she was. Nobody would guess she was pregnant; of course Nora already knew, but she hadn't said anything yet. There was no reason for anyone to believe she was expecting, so worrying over her fuller chest was ridiculous.

Still, she feared that when the rest of her family found out, when her *father* found out she was not only expecting, but carrying a Newport child, there would be trouble. She'd already gotten a glimpse of things to come from Nora. Her family wouldn't be happy. Granted, she was going into this situation with her eyes wide open and not full of stars. Eve had lost a child before when she thought herself in love. Now her family would probably criticize her for making a mistake with another man who was all wrong for her.

Not that her baby was a mistake; the first person to even hint at that would have to deal with her wrath. No, her mistakes came in the form of choosing the wrong men. Clearly she had bad judgment.

By the time Eve pulled onto the Winchester estate, she was confident that she needed to tell her family. The sooner they knew about the baby, the longer they'd have to get used to the idea. After the party tonight, she'd tell Grace and their father when they were all together. It would be the perfect time. Not that there was a perfect time to drop a bomb like this. But there was no changing the fact that she was having a baby.

A baby. The thought thrilled and terrified her at the same time. She was still ten weeks away from the seventeen-week mark. She would feel so much better once she got past the hurdle that had left a hole in her heart during her last pregnancy. Eve honestly didn't know if she could bear another loss so great. She was already facing the inevitable loss of her father, but to add a second baby to the…

No. This baby was just fine. She wasn't going to even think that way… From now on she would have only positive thoughts. Her child was a Newport and a Winchester, which immediately equaled a fighter.

Eve pulled in behind Grace's car and grabbed her clutch and the present she'd brought for her father—a framed photograph. Sliding her phone into her purse, Eve headed toward the grand entrance. Her childhood home was nothing short of spectacular—Sutton Winchester would settle for nothing less than the best.

Instantly memories of growing up here flooded her mind. The house always looked like a museum, but there had been a toy room on the third floor where the kids were given free rein. She and her sisters had spent hours in there playing, dreaming, fighting…all the things close sisters did. They'd run around outside playing tag, chasing each other and fantasizing about being grown-ups. Seriously, growing up was so overrated. They should've enjoyed those carefree days a bit more.

Pulling her wrap tighter around her, Eve made her way to the door. Without knocking, she let herself in. The aroma of something spicy, maybe cinnamon, hit her. Definitely a hint of pumpkin, too. Whatever the cook had prepared—or Nora had had catered—smelled absolutely divine. And thankfully in the evenings, Eve was fine; she didn't have to deal with a queasy belly. So she was ready to have her fill of the party food, but not the wine.

Eve had just pulled her wrap off to hang it on the coat tree in the foyer when Nora came gliding down the hall. Eve put her wrap up and set her clutch and gift on the marble entryway table.

"You look gorgeous," her younger sister declared. "I knew this goddess costume would be so perfect for you."

Eve took in her sister's vibrant green historical ball gown. "Talk about stunning. Nora, you're glowing."

Nora beamed. "I know it's not what I bought

when we were out, but then I saw this the other day and had to have it."

"So what is Reid?"

"Lucky." Eve glanced at Reid, who'd just stepped from the formal living space. He wrapped an arm around Nora's waist and kissed her cheek. "I'm damn lucky," he added.

Reid was dressed as a Civil War–era soldier, complete with sword dangling at his side. He and Nora looked as though they'd stepped out of a time machine. Eve was jealous of Nora's itty-bitty waist; no doubt she'd gone for the whole corset and all. Eve's hourglass shape was not long for this world.

"That you are," Eve agreed, giving her sister a wink. "How's Dad feeling today?"

"Good. He's even donned a bit of a costume for the occasion, though he said he'd stay in the study since his oxygen and everything is set up in there. Visitors are welcome, though."

Eve gripped the present beneath her arm and nodded. "I'm going to see him now before everyone else arrives."

"You doing okay?" Nora asked, keeping the question vague.

Eve glanced at Reid, who showed no sign of knowing anything. "I'm great. If you'll excuse me."

Eve made her way to the study. She hated thinking of her father being so sick that he was confined to one room, but she knew that if he truly wanted to move about the house, his caregivers would make it happen. Her father remained in the study more out of pride than anything else. There was a bathroom right off the spacious room and hospice care had set everything up to look like a master suite. Her father's old desk where he'd spent countless hours when he worked from home sat in the corner. Next to the desk was a large built-in shelf housing all of his favorite books.

As she walked down the hall, Eve took stock of all the memories. She hated the thought of his estate being split up when he passed. She wanted her childhood home to remain in the family, but that might not be possible. Who knew what would happen with Carson and how far his brothers would go to make sure he received his share.

Just the thought of Graham stirred mixed emotions within Eve. The ache she had for him kept growing with each day that passed without him, but on the other hand, she hated knowing he was one of the forces waging war against her father.

Pulling the framed picture from beneath her arm, Eve tapped lightly on the double doors and let herself into the study. The cozy fire welcomed her. Her father was actually in his chair beside the flickering flames. The last time she'd visited, he'd been sitting up in bed but hadn't felt like going much farther. To see him in a chair was such a surprise, Eve's eyes instantly filled with tears. The eye patch and pirate hat combined with his navy blue bathrobe made her laugh, though. He'd dressed up for the guests that would come through. If it weren't for the oxygen, she'd swear he was back to normal. But he'd never be himself again. He'd never be the man he once was and she was slowly coming to grips with the harsh reality.

"Look at this beautiful goddess who came to visit." He lifted a hand toward her. "Come on over. You look stunning, Eve. Just like your mother."

Of course she looked like her mother; everyone told her as much growing up. The honey-brown hair, the bright eyes, curvy figure. Eve had seen enough pictures of her mother in her younger years to know she was practically a clone. But Eve didn't want to discuss her mother right now. She wanted this evening to be fun, to be filled with love since the entire family would all be under one roof.

"What have you got?"

Eve flipped the frame around. "I had this made for you. It's from my visit the other day."

Sutton stared at the picture for several moments before finally reaching for it. With both hands, he gripped the sleek pewter frame and settled it on his lap. Eve waited, watching as her father continued to look at the faces staring back at him. Sutton with his daughters, an image that hadn't been captured since they were little.

"This means everything to me," he said, his voice thick with emotion. "You've always had such a good eye for photos."

Eve leaned against the side of the chair and

laughed. "It was just a selfie, Dad. But I thought it turned out nice and wanted you to have something in your room."

He glanced up at her, his bushy brows drawn together. "You always know what to do. This is perfect."

"I'm glad you like it."

He looked at the image once more before turning his attention back to her. "Tell me about Elite. How are things going?"

The man was on his deathbed and wanted to know about business. He would probably die with his company—his baby—on his mind.

"We're doing great." Eve was thrilled with the direction they'd taken since she'd been placed at the helm. "We actually just signed on a Sydney office two days ago."

Sutton's smile spread across his face. "I knew you would take a great company and make it even greater. I'm so proud of you, Eve. You've not let anything stand in your way."

"I learned from the best," she declared, wrapping her arm around his shoulders as she settled a hip on the arm of his chair.

"Some women are cut out for husbands, kids, which is fine. But I knew you were the one to follow in my footsteps. You never had—"

"Let's not talk about work." She had to steer him in another direction. Because even though she hadn't wanted the whole family lifestyle once she'd gotten a taste of corporate world, clearly she wasn't going to be able to dodge it for long. "Nora said you were feeling pretty well today. You look good."

He started to laugh, but his robust chuckle quickly turned into a coughing fit. Eve rushed to the wet bar in the corner and refilled his water. She hated seeing him suffer even the slightest bit. For a man who was known to be a ruthless shark in the real estate world, he was now as weak as a baby. The vulnerable side of Sutton Winchester would only be known to his family, though. He'd never let outsiders see him in such shape.

Eve let him hold the cup while she took the framed picture and set it up on the table near the sofa.

"Thank you," he said after taking a few sips. "Damn disease."

Eve went back to his side and took his cup. She placed it on the small table next to him.

"You girls don't have to lie to me," he went on, taking her hand and squeezing it between both of his. "I know what I look like."

Eve kissed the top of his head. "Like my handsome father."

"You're going to find some man and charm him one day," her father teased. "Just make sure when you do that you don't leave my company in a bind."

As if she'd ever settle down and take the time to nurture a relationship. A global company and a new baby were definitely enough to keep her occupied. "I'll never leave Elite," she promised.

"I hate to bring this up—"

"But you will because you're honest," she joked. "Go ahead."

"I know that before all the questions came up about me being the Newport boys' father, you and Graham were—"

"Nothing," Eve interrupted. "We were nothing." And that was the truth. It was *after* the paternity test results came back that they tore each other's clothes off.

This conversation was entering dangerous territory, and that was putting it mildly. Guilt squeezed her chest like a vise. There was no way to avoid it much longer, but she wasn't going to tell anyone about the baby until after the party. No way was she going to ruin Nora and Reid's evening. There would be enough time to discuss it after the guests were gone and only family remained.

"I saw how he looked at you, Eve," her father went on. "Getting involved with a Newport would be the biggest mistake you could make."

Eve bit the inside of her cheek to keep from saying anything. What could she say? She could deny that she was involved, but that would be an obvious lie. She could even pretend they weren't going to be anything more than parents sharing a child, but since they were still flirting and she couldn't get him off her mind, it was only a matter of time before her control crumbled and they ended up intimate again.

Pulling her hand from her father's grasp, she

leaned down once more and kissed his head. "I'm going to go see if Nora needs help since the guests should be arriving any minute. I'll be back in a bit."

To tell you I'm expecting a Newport's baby.

"You'd better," her father winked. "But keep in mind what I said, Eve. Graham and Brooks have an agenda. They think I know their father's name and they'll use any means necessary to get it. I wouldn't put it past him to use you to get to me."

Eve stilled. She'd never thought for a second that Graham was using her for anything other than a bedmate…and she'd used him right back. But did her father's words hold any truth? Nora had hinted at the same thing the other day. Was her family just being overly cautious or did they truly believe Graham would use her to get to Sutton?

No. Graham wasn't the type of man to play games. He was a lethal attorney and when he wanted something, he went straight at it. He wasn't the type of man to hide behind a woman and let her do the work.

Eve let herself back out into the hallway and pulled in a deep breath. Voices filtered through the house and it was clear guests had started arriving. Giving her cleavage one last glance in a mirror, she gave a mental shrug and headed toward the formal living room.

Grace, Nora and Reid stood near the mantel, talking and laughing. Grace was dressed as a sexy witch with glittery hose, a sparkly black hat and some killer black stilettos. Their guests were dressed in various fun costumes. Eve glanced around the room and saw an oversize Mrs. Potato Head—presumably the Mr. Potato Head by the wet bar with an appetizer in his hand was the spouse. There was another couple dressed as Vikings and a few others in glamorous gowns and masks. Some reminded her of Mardi Gras with their ribbons and gems.

Eve was stopped by Lucinda Wilde and Josh Calhoun. Lucinda was their father's main caretaker and had pretty much morphed into being one of the family. She and Josh had fallen in love recently and Eve smiled as the couple approached her.

"If there's a contest for best costumes, you two win hands down."

Lucinda smiled as Josh wrapped his arm around her waist. "Josh isn't one for dressing up, so he basically threw on things he already owned."

Eve gave him an approving nod. "The cowboy look works. And your saloon girl is perfect," she told Lucinda. "I could never pull that off, but you guys look so authentic."

"I'm here for the food," Josh joked as he tipped his hat down in a typical cowboy fashion. "And I'd use any excuse to have Lucinda dress up like this."

Lucinda gave him a playful swat. "Eve, you look amazing. This is such a fun party, and I think it's just what Sutton needs. He may come out later."

"Really?" Eve asked. "I hope he does. Everyone here loves him and I know it would do him good."

"I agree," Lucinda said. "I'm going to talk to him in a bit and coerce him to join the party. I even dressed him up."

"I saw," Eve laughed. "I love the pirate."

"It's all he would agree to."

Lucinda glanced around the room, pushing her curls to the side so they slid over one bare shoulder. "If you'll excuse me, I'd like to talk to Nora and Reid. They look great, too."

Eve watched as the two couples met in the middle of the room. They laughed and chatted. Eve stared for a moment too long because she caught Grace's curious look and quirked brow, silently asking if Eve was okay.

Eve pasted on a smile and gave a brief nod. Everything was fine. Seriously. Just because she was expecting a child by a man who was an enemy of her father, just because the two families would go ballistic once the pregnancy was revealed, and just because her father was dying…why shouldn't she be fine?

Thirteen

She needed air desperately. The more guests that filled the house, the more Eve felt as though she was suffocating. She'd spent over an hour smiling, making small talk and wondering if anyone noticed how she kept her water glass full and ignored the wine.

The Winchester mansion was vast, but still, the walls had been closing in on her.

Escaping out the back patio doors, Eve slid off her gold sandals and padded barefoot around the pool. The stones were cool on her feet and for once she welcomed the brisk breeze. She'd started getting so warm inside, but then her body temperature had been off lately. *Thank you, hormones.*

When an arm snaked around her waist, Eve gasped.

"It's me," a familiar voice whispered in her ear.

Her entire body tingled at the warm breath against the side of her face, the taut chest against her back. But as much as she relished the feel of Graham against her, fear gripped her. "What are you doing here?" she whispered.

"My invitation got lost in the mail."

Eve smiled, but quickly composed herself before turning in his arms. "You're—"

Words died on her lips when she realized he was wearing a mask...one of those Mardi Gras masks she'd seen a few of the guests wearing earlier. And a tux. Mercy sakes he had on a tuxedo and looked just as perfectly packaged as he had the night of the charity ball.

Graham slid the mask over his head and took her hand. Without a word he pulled her toward the pool house. A thrill of excitement rushed through her as Graham tried the knob and it turned beneath his palm.

He ushered her inside, closed the door and left the lights off. She waited for him to devour her, to run his hands over her heated body. But nothing. Her eyes hadn't adjusted to the darkness and she couldn't see him.

"Graham?"

"I'm right here."

His voice was close. The heat from his body had her shifting, hoping to brush against him...waiting for him to make contact somehow.

"What are you doing?" she asked.

"I told you, my invitation got lost in the mail."

Eve rolled her eyes, even though he couldn't see her. "No. What are you doing in here?"

Material rustled. Something, his sleeve maybe, brushed against the back of her hand then was instantly gone. Her body was wound so tight in anticipation of his touch. What was he waiting on?

"I wanted to see you," he said in that low tone that had shivers racing through her. "You sent me that picture and I knew I had to find a way to be at this party."

"Did anyone—"

"No. Nobody saw me. I even talked to a few guests, but no one caught on."

Relief washed over her, but was quickly replaced once again by arousal. "Are you...why are we..."

"Are you achy, Eve?"

That sultry voice filled the darkness. Her eyes were finally starting to adjust somewhat, but there were no outside lights coming in because the entrance to the pool house faced the back of the property. Damn it. She wanted to see him better, to touch him. What game was he playing?

"Have you thought of me these past few days?" he continued. "I know you have or you wouldn't be sending me pictures of you in that sexy costume. Did you think I'd come begging for you? I told you, you'd be the one begging."

She was damn near ready to do just that. "Is that

why you're here? To get me to beg?" she asked, hoping her voice sounded stronger than she felt.

"I'm here because I told you I wanted to be your date."

Eve eased away from the door, only to stop short when she ran into Graham's hard chest. "So what are we doing in the pool house?" she asked, holding her hands up to steady herself. She couldn't stop herself from gliding her palms up the tux jacket toward his broad shoulders.

"Your call, Eve. I told you I won't be the one to make a move."

Why did life have to be full of so many tempting choices? Why was her greatest need the exact opposite of what she should be doing? But the lengths he went to in order to be with her was rather...oh, fine. It was flat-out arousing and exciting.

"You're quite cocky to come into my family's home," she told him, roaming her hands up toward his neck, her fingertips teasing that smooth jawline.

"Call it what you want, but there was no way in hell I was going to let some damn picture pacify my need for you."

He'd never admitted he needed her before. Granted he was talking in physical terms, but the words still sent a thrill of desire through her.

Eve leaned in until her lips barely brushed against his. "So you're here to give in after all? Dare I say, beg me?" she whispered.

With a groan, Graham snaked his arms around

her waist and gripped her backside, pulling her flush against him. "Hell no. I'm not begging. I'm taking what I want, what you've teased me with, and I'm saving your pride so *you* don't have to beg."

Eve laughed. "So this is all for me?"

"I'm a selfish man, Eve. Never forget that."

His lips crushed hers as he backed her up a few steps to the door. She hit with a thud, but she barely noticed. With the way Graham's hands were wrestling the hem of her dress up her thighs, she couldn't concentrate on anything but the endless possibilities of what was about to happen.

"Never tease me again," Graham muttered against her lips. "Did you think I'd avoid you, knowing you looked like this?"

His mouth made a path down her neck, to the deep V of her dress. For the first time tonight, she was all too happy to be this exposed. Better access for Graham was exactly what she needed, what she ached for.

Eve arched her back, cupping the side of his face as he jerked the thick straps down her shoulders. The second her dress fell to her waist, Graham filled his hands with her bare breasts.

"If I'd known you weren't wearing anything beneath this, I would've intercepted you at your house before the party and we never would've left."

Eve gasped as his lips found her sensitive tip. "The dress…it has…um…"

"Yes?" he asked, a smile in his tone. "How close are you to begging?"

About a second.

"The dress has a built-in liner. No bra necessary."

"It's my new favorite."

When his hands trailed up the back of her thighs, Eve had to bite her lips to keep from crying out. He knew every single place to touch her and have her squirming. He knew she was on the brink of begging and he was practically gloating over it.

Time to turn the tables, so to speak.

Eve reached between them. The second she stroked her hand up his length, Graham let out a hiss.

"I'm not playing games, Eve."

She couldn't help but smile against his mouth. "You wouldn't have come here if you weren't playing."

She. Was. Killing. Him.

And his slow descent had started the second she'd sent that picture of her wearing the dress. But, seeing her in person, touching those curves, was absolutely everything he'd ever dreamed and fantasized about. Yes, he'd had her multiple times, but knowing she was carrying his child bumped up the sexual appeal. There was something so primal, so...damn it, *his*. She was his. That child was his. There would never be another man coming into her life, into their child's life. Not so long as Graham was around.

Maybe he'd come here to seduce her, most likely. But he'd intentionally decided to crash the party simply because he knew he could. He'd taken matters into his own hands.

Speaking of matters in hand…

"Take off your dress."

Eve stilled. "Here?"

"We can go back inside to the party to do this, but I'm sure your family wouldn't approve."

Graham backed away and waited until the rustling and soft swoosh of fabric indicated she was indeed bare for him. Closing the space between them, Graham wasted no time in grabbing hold of her and lifting her until her legs wrapped around him.

He eased over slightly so her back wasn't against the grooves in the door. But once he had her against the wall, he reached between them, unfastened his pants and kissed her. Hard. This wasn't a sweet encounter; he didn't have time for gentle touches and nurturing words. He was in this dark pool house with his own goddess for one reason only.

"Hurry," she panted against his mouth.

Clearly Eve was in here for one reason, as well. This was why they got along so well. Their needs, their wants were identical in nearly every single way. Convincing her to be his wife would be the easiest case he'd ever made.

The soft pants, the occasional groan from Eve were begging enough. Graham slid into her, smiling when her fingers curled around his shoulders and gripped tighter. The way she whispered his name as she threw her head back and closed her eyes only fueled Graham to move faster.

"It's been too long," he growled as he kept a firm hold on her hips. "Never again."

"No," she murmured, her eyes locking with his.

Graham couldn't go another day without touching her, let alone several. His stupid pride and the ridiculous game he'd played…it had backfired in his face. Now he was the one needing her, but damn if he'd admit it.

"I'm the only one, Eve." He didn't know why he needed to express this, but damn if another man would be keeping her bed warm. For now, she was his. "Say it."

Nodding, she gasped when he pushed harder. "The only one. Only you."

Feeling too vulnerable, way too close to the edge of exposing feelings he wasn't ready to come face-to-face with, Graham angled his mouth across hers once more. His hips quickened, and her knees tightened around his waist.

When her hands came up to frame his face, Graham ignored the tingle of awareness. He wanted it fast, hard, intense. Little sweet gestures weren't for him. They weren't for *them*.

Eve tore her mouth from his and squeezed her eyes tight.

"No. Look at me," he demanded. His eyes had

adjusted to the darkness and he wanted to see as much of her as possible.

When her body convulsed, Graham could no longer hold back. He buried his face in the side of her neck, inhaling that familiar, jasmine scent. Holding tight, he waited until their bodies ceased trembling before he lifted his face. Her heart beat so fast against his chest, matching his own frantic pace.

"My family is going to wonder where I went," Eve murmured, breaking the silence.

Graham nipped at her lips. "Tell them you needed some fresh air."

"I don't even want to look in a mirror. They're going to wonder why I'm so messed up."

"Then leave with me."

Why had he said that? They weren't inseparable. But there was something about knowing they shared this baby…the bond was already too strong. Graham needed to rein things back in or he was going to find himself in a position he wasn't ready for.

Eve slid her legs from his waist. "We'll both pretend you didn't say that."

Once she was standing and had her balance, Graham stepped back and adjusted his clothes. He'd barely taken the edge off and if he stayed at this party, he was going to have to find a spare bathroom or walk-in closet to drag her into.

He pulled out his phone to use as a light, shining it on Eve. The instant the glow hit her face, she froze and blinked at him. But it was the tousled hair, the swollen lips and pinkened cheeks that held him captivated. There was no denying what she'd been up to and the thought of her putting that dress back on while looking so rumpled sent a jolt of desire through him.

"I can't see your face with that light in my eyes," she told him, holding up a hand. "But if I don't get back in there, my family is going to worry."

Angling his phone toward her body as she pulled her dress back up, Graham reached a hand out to help her. "I'm going in, too. I'm not going to leave."

"Why would you want to stay?"

Because he wanted to touch her, he wanted to catch a glimpse of her across the room…because apparently he was a masochist. Mostly because she was trying to push him away when she clearly didn't mean it, and he wouldn't let her.

"Because I can," he said simply.

Once she'd adjusted her dress, she pushed her hair back behind her shoulders. "I'm going to tell the rest of my family about the baby after the party."

He tightened his hold on his phone. No. He had to get her to agree to marriage before she told her family. They would instantly tell her what a mistake it was to be involved with him. They'd get inside her head and have her doubting.

"Are you sure that's a smart move? They already think I'm using you."

"Are you?"

He couldn't blame her for asking. Apparently

they'd already gotten to her. "If you thought I was, you wouldn't be in here with me," he countered. He hadn't used her, not by any means. But now that she was having his baby, he would marry her to ensure that their child had a Newport name. A detail she didn't need to know.

Yes, he could've used her to get to her father, but he hadn't. Didn't that count for something?

"Regardless of what they think, they need to know," Eve continued. "There's so much worry with my father, fear of the unknown, and now with Carson finding out he's our half brother. My family needs to know exactly what they're dealing with. Besides, maybe this baby will be the bond that brings our families together and resolves this ridiculous feud."

Graham wasn't so sure of that, but if she wanted to tell them, he'd support her…after that ring was on her finger.

"Let's wait a few days," he said, holding up a hand when she opened her mouth. "I want you to come away with me."

"What?"

Yeah, what did he mean? Where had that come from? He hadn't planned it. But now that he'd offered the trip, he had to admit it was a brilliant plan.

"We'll go away for just a couple days," he hurried on. "Nobody has to know, and when we get back, you and I can tell them."

"I'm telling them tonight, Graham. I've waited long enough."

Her inflexible tone told him this battle would be more difficult than he'd thought.

"I need to get back inside," she told him.

"I'm coming in, too."

Eve hesitated, but finally nodded. "Just keep your mask on until after the party, okay? I'd hate to have a scene with so many people here."

Graham would love nothing more than to cause a scene, but out of respect for Eve, he'd keep the mask on. He searched the floor, then found it. After sliding it back into place, he bowed toward her.

"You go on," he told her. "I'll be in later. You won't even know I'm there."

With her hand on the knob, she threw him a glance over her shoulder. "I'll know you're there. I'll feel you."

With those parting words, she was gone.

She'd *feel* him? Of course she would. And even across the room, he'd undoubtedly feel her, as well. The line he'd been teetering on, swearing he wouldn't cross it, was starting to waver. He was losing his grip and it was only a matter of time before he lost his balance and fell face-first into emotions he'd purposely dodged.

This entire situation was messy and if he wasn't careful, someone was going to end up hurt.

Fourteen

No matter how she mingled with the guests, no matter how many jokes Reid told her and no matter how many times she refilled her glass of sparkling water, Eve felt the presence of Graham just the same as if he'd come up and wrapped his arms around her.

Nora and Reid separated, but kept making eye contact with each other. Eve wondered what that kind of connection would be like. To look across the room and have your soul mate watching you. Silent communication passed between the couple. Whatever they were sharing, Reid gave a nod and Nora moved through the crowd toward the front of the formal living room.

"Those two are up to something," Grace whispered behind Eve's back. "They've been sneaking around all evening."

Eve caught sight of Graham across the room in the familiar mask. His face was turned toward hers, but she couldn't see his eyes. No matter, she knew they were on her. The connection across the room… it was just like Nora and Reid's.

No. She and Graham were nothing like her sister and Reid. Were they?

"That's what lovers do," Eve replied, not taking her gaze from Graham. She had to admit, the thrill of having him in her family home was exciting. For someone who was such a stickler for rules, lately she found herself not caring so long as she saw Graham.

No matter how she tried to shift her focus to the baby, to remain in control of her life, she kept getting pulled back into Graham's web. The encounter in the pool house shouldn't have happened, but she wouldn't change anything. How could she keep denying what they both wanted? They were having a baby together. That didn't mean they had to automatically stop seeing each other…did it?

Nerves fluttered in her stomach. She was anxious to get this night over with, to finally let her family know what was going on. If there was an issue, she'd deal with it, but she couldn't keep living this secret life. Keeping her affair hidden was difficult enough, but there was no way she'd be able to keep a child from her family. Soon, very soon, they'd see the evidence.

"Can I have everybody's attention?" Reid called. When only half the room quieted, he put his fingers to his mouth and whistled. Silence immediately settled over the space. "I'd like your attention."

"What's going on?" Eve asked her younger sister.

"No idea, but Dad was just wheeled in."

Eve turned around. Dr. Wilde was heading their way with their father. Sutton had his eyes on Eve and Grace, a smile on his pale face. The cancer had robbed him of his color, his dignity and his normal life. But here he was, attending the party in costume, giving his terminal illness the middle finger.

Eve glanced at Dr. Wilde, then down at her father when he pulled up beside her in his wheelchair and reached for her hand to give it a quick squeeze.

"Nora and Reid asked if I'd come in," he explained.

Reid cleared his throat, drawing Eve's attention back toward the front of the room. "As many of you know, Nora and I have been seeing each other for some time now. I've fallen in love with her, with her son, and I want to make things official."

Nora's wide smile was infectious. Eve found herself grinning, knowing what was coming. She clasped her hands in front of her mouth, mostly to prevent people from seeing her chin quiver. She was so emotional lately.

"I've asked Nora to marry me." Cheers erupted in the room. "I've also asked to adopt her son," Reid went on. Wrapping an arm around Nora's waist, he pulled her flush against his side. "She said yes and we plan to be married on Thanksgiving right here on the Winchester estate."

A burst of applause, and congratulations filled the room. Grace squealed and headed for the happy couple. Eve looked down at her father, who had actually teared up. Apparently she wasn't the only one with high emotions lately.

"You didn't know?" Eve asked.

"I had an idea. She asked if she could host a family gathering on Thanksgiving and I told her that would be great and just what the family needed."

Eve gestured to Lucinda, who was standing behind the wheelchair. "One of us will take him back in a bit. Go mingle."

With a simple nod, Lucinda made her way toward Josh. Eve gripped the chair and pushed her father toward Reid and Nora. Once Nora spotted their dad, she rushed forward, arms wide.

"I hope this is okay, Dad." She threw her arms around him before leaning back to search his face. "I wanted to surprise everyone, to ease some of the tension this family has been dealing with from the trouble with the Newports and your illness."

At the mention of the Newports, Eve searched for Graham, but couldn't find him. Surely he hadn't left. He wouldn't. Somewhere he was waiting for his chance to get her alone again.

"This is perfect, Nora," their father said. "I'm so

happy for you guys and having the wedding here is an excellent idea."

Nora straightened and said to Eve, "I hope you'll stand up by my side."

Eve hugged her sister. "I wouldn't be anywhere else."

When Nora pulled away, she looked toward Eve's flat stomach, then back up into her eyes. "Everything okay?"

Eve simply nodded, not wanting to get into this now.

Dread filled her. No, she couldn't get into this now, or even an hour from now. This night belonged to Nora and Reid. The baby news would definitely have to wait, but for how long? As much as Eve would love to shield her child from the fallout, she knew she'd have to just tell her family and not worry about the timing. But telling them right now was definitely out of the question.

Stealing the night from Nora and Reid wasn't right.

A flash from the corner of her eye had her turning. The man in the striking Mardi Gras mask moved toward her. There was no way Graham could get this close to her family. He wouldn't purposely give away his identity, but still the idea of him getting within talking distance had Eve excusing herself from her sisters and father.

"You need to go," she whispered as she walked by him.

Eve kept walking, knowing he was right behind her. When they reached the foyer, Eve smiled at one of Nora's friends who was heading down the hall toward the bathroom.

Once the foyer was empty, Graham lifted his mask to rest it on the top of his head. With his back to the rest of the house, he stared down at her. He wasn't too concerned about the risk of being seen, not with the way he was standing.

"I can't tell them," Eve murmured. "Not tonight."

She hated this. Hated that such an innocent child, a child she loved with all her heart, was being kept a secret like there was something…dirty. A child should be celebrated, not hidden.

Graham's hands slid up her bare arms, his fingers curled over her shoulders. "I know."

He pulled her into his embrace and Eve willingly went. She hated leaning on anyone, but right now, they were a team, whether either of them wanted to admit it or not. And she had to admit, having Graham's arms around her felt…right. But that couldn't be. Nothing about having him here, let alone his embracing her as if he cared, was right. This affair had started as a whirlwind and they were caught up, that's all. There could be nothing more.

"Let's go away," he whispered into her ear. "We'll go to my cabin in Tennessee for a few days and relax. Nothing will bother us, you can rest, and we can figure out a plan that will work for our child and our families."

Was that even possible? She'd give anything to be able to escape for a few days, to come to terms with everything and figure out a way to work with Graham. But if she went away with him, she knew what that meant…there would be more of what had transpired in the pool house.

Eve sighed and pulled back. "My mind is all over the place." She glanced over his shoulder to make sure they were still alone. "Let's go out onto the porch."

Once they were outside, she led him down to where the lights weren't shining right on them. The chilly air hit her hard and Graham instantly took off his black jacket and draped it around her shoulders. His familiar woodsy scent hit her, and the warmth from the jacket where it had hugged his body was just like having his arms around her.

"I keep battling myself where you're concerned," she went on, gripping the lapels closer together. "I want to keep my distance physically, but then I see you and—"

"I don't even have to see you to want you."

"Graham, we have to think of what's best here."

"I am." He leaned in closer, crowding her against the side of the house. "Right now, I'm thinking that escaping for a few days is exactly what we need. We would have time to talk without interruptions. I can fly the helicopter and nobody would have to know where you and I went. We'll both just say we're away on business."

Eve closed her eyes, giving the idea more thought than she probably should. "You make this seem so simple."

"Say the word and I'll make sure it's simple," he whispered against her mouth. "All you'll have to do is pack a bag."

There was a reason Graham was one of the top lawyers in Chicago. The man could persuade anyone with that charm of his. He made his case so perfectly, so convincingly. Eve opened her eyes, meeting his bright blue stare.

"When do we leave?"

"You're leaving when?"

Graham held the phone between his shoulder and his ear. "Tonight."

Brooks laughed on the other end of the line. "Who is she?"

After placing a perfectly folded pair of jeans in his carry-on bag, Graham stood straight up and gripped the phone. "I said it was work related."

"We pretty much have the same mind and I know this urgency in your tone has nothing to do with work."

Hell, yeah, he was urgent to get Eve alone in his cabin. The obvious reason of privacy aside, Eve needed rest, she needed to relax and not worry about telling her family she was expecting. Now that Nora knew, Graham prayed she was too focused on her engagement to discuss Eve's condition. Graham had to trust her to keep her word. Plus, he had an engagement of his own to worry about. He wanted to get that ring on Eve's finger, and he'd use this trip to advance his case.

"I have a pressing matter that needs my attention," Graham said to his twin. "I'll only be gone three days."

"And this has to do with what case?" Brooks asked in a mocking tone.

"You know I can't discuss my client cases with you." Totally true. "Besides, I need to finish packing, so this conversation is over. Unless there's an emergency, don't contact me and I'll let you know when I get home."

"If I find out our father's name I'll sure as hell be calling you and you'll have to put your mystery woman on hold."

"If you find out our father's name, I'll be back," Graham promised.

"Wait…tell me you're not sneaking out of town with Eve. I thought you were done messing with her."

Graham turned toward his walk-in closet to grab some shirts. "I'm not messing around with anyone."

It was only partly a lie. Because he wasn't messing with her. He was the father of her child. That went well beyond messing.

"You're lying, but I'll let you off the hook because I'm on my way to meet Roman. He thinks he has a lead. I'll keep you posted."

"This late?" Graham asked.

"He texted me right before you called, so whatever he wants, it must be something important."

Excitement filled Graham as the possibilities swirled through his head. "Did he say what the lead was?"

"No. And he said it was minor, but at this point we're going to explore any option we have."

Graham would love nothing more than to find their biological father. Then maybe Brooks's vendetta against Sutton would ease up a bit and the tension would ease between their families. But that was doubtful, especially when Sutton discovered Eve was pregnant.

"Keep me posted," Graham told his brother before hanging up.

After tossing in the rest of his belongings, Graham zipped up the bag. He couldn't wait to get Eve to the cabin. She could take long bubble baths in the garden tub in the master suite that overlooked the mountains and just relax. He would make sure of it. He'd already called one of his staff members to have certain foods stocked. Eve wouldn't want for a thing these next few days.

The only look he wanted to see on her face was happiness. She was still so early in her pregnancy, and his goal was to get her to take her mind off her troubles because he knew she was worried.

Which left the question he'd had on his mind for days. What did Nora mean when she'd mentioned

Eve's previous pregnancy? Graham didn't want to dredge up bad memories for her, but he also felt he deserved to know.

These three days could bring anything their way. But one thing was for sure: Graham wasn't going to let her get away without convincing her to marry him. This child would be a Newport. Added to that, merging the families in such a bold way would show everyone just how serious they were about ending this feud. But time was running out and Graham needed to act fast.

He grabbed his things and set the security alarm on his penthouse. After he swung by to pick up Eve, they'd be on their way to his cabin. Nothing would stop him from putting that ring on her finger. He may not have been looking for a family, but there was no way in hell another man would raise his child. And he'd yet to find anyone as compatible as Eve. No, they weren't in love, but what did that have to do with marriages these days anyway? Being an attorney, he'd seen the aftermath when people entered into holy matrimony solely on the basis of love. *No thank you.*

Graham was confident that by the end of this trip, he'd have Eve convinced this was the best decision for everyone. He knew what to say, how to get her to see his side. After all, he'd gotten her to agree to this trip in no time.

A little seduction, a little charm and she'd have that ring on her finger.

Fifteen

A cabin? Who referred to a sprawling five-thousand-square-foot log home as a cabin?

Being the real estate guru she was, Eve nearly laughed when she saw Graham's home away from home. The place was stunning and she hadn't even walked in the front door yet. It was after midnight, so she couldn't see the views. But the old lantern-style lights on the porch illuminated a beautiful facade and had her anxious to see the inside.

"I've got your bag."

Eve stood at the bottom of the stone steps leading up to the entrance. She'd forgotten all about her things once Graham had opened her car door and she'd seen the beauty of this place. All she wanted to do was take in each and every detail because she knew she'd never be back. She couldn't wait for sunrise. She'd bet money the views were spectacular.

"Ready to go inside?" he asked.

Eve blinked, glancing over at him. He held both bags and offered her a smile she knew she wouldn't be able to resist later.

Was she ready to go in? Was she ready to spend three days with a man she was falling for? Was she ready to let him fully into her life, into her heart? She'd made the decision last night after the party to come clean about her feelings. Graham needed to know. There could be no secrets between them, not if she wanted a chance at making this work.

"I'm ready," she told him.

The wide porch had sturdy wooden swings at each end that swayed in the gentle breeze. The warmer temperature here seemed so inviting and Eve already made mental plans to take advantage of those swings. She'd come to relax and she intended to do just that.

"I have the refrigerator stocked with your favorite foods," Graham told her as he set the bags at his feet so he could unlock the door. "I did a search on foods you couldn't have while pregnant, so no swordfish for you."

Eve laughed. "And here I was hoping you'd show me what you could do in the kitchen with swordfish."

That got a chuckle out of him. "I have something else planned for our meals."

The way he threw a sultry look over his shoulder told her he had more than dinner planned…not that she didn't know that already. Even after being with him so many times, she still anticipated their three days together. Something about being here, being so isolated from the outside, plus being so far from their families, seemed even more intimate. Yes, they were still sneaking, but for the next three days, they could be themselves.

Eve stopped short before she could enter the house. After all they'd been through, this would be the first time they actually slept together. They'd both been careful about not sleeping over—that would've been another level they hadn't discussed. But here, she had to assume they were sharing a room.

Maybe not, though. Maybe he'd put her stuff in a guest room. If that were the case, then the feelings she wanted to reveal would be a moot point.

Eve knew one thing. By the end of this trip, they were going to have to have some serious plans laid out because she couldn't handle this emotional upheaval anymore.

The second Graham swung the old oak door open, Eve gasped. The open floor plan gave an immediate view all the way through the house. But that wasn't the extraordinary part. The opposite wall was nothing but a showcase of floor-to-ceiling windows overlooking the mountains and valleys. The lights dotting the landscape were so sporadic, so different from Chicago. There was space to breathe here, nature to explore. This was exactly the escape she needed from the city, from the chaos in her life.

As if pulled toward the beauty, Eve slowly crossed the open space. "Whatever you paid for this place was worth it."

Graham laughed as she passed him. "I had the same reaction when I first opened the door, too. I knew the asking price was high, but the second I saw that view, I knew this place would be mine."

Eve threw a glance over her shoulder. "And is that how things normally work for you? You see something you want and take it?"

He let the bags he was carrying fall to the floor with a thunk. "Always."

The intensity of his stare combined with his instant response had Eve turning back toward the million-dollar view. She already knew Graham was a go-getter; it was one of the qualities she found most attractive in him.

The way he'd been protective of her feelings, of her emotions during the party earlier had sealed the deal, though. She'd gone and fallen for Graham Newport, father of her child. Even if the baby didn't exist, Eve wouldn't have been able to stop herself.

But they *had* created a child.

A flashback to a time during her previous pregnancy when her belly had been slightly rounded hit Eve as she placed a hand over her stomach. She longed to feel a baby move beneath her palm, wanted to know there was a healthy child thriving inside of her.

Hands slid over her shoulders. "What are you thinking?"

Eve leaned back against Graham's firm chest. Did she open up to him? Did she fully let him in? If she wanted a chance at this, then yes. But not right now. She didn't want to start these relaxing days by dumping the darkest memories of her life right in his lap.

"Something to be saved for another time," she told him.

One of his hands came down to slide over hers. "No worrying. Remember?"

"I'm trying."

Graham spun her around, framed her face and kissed her softly. "Why don't you look around and I'll work on getting something to eat? I know you barely ate at the party."

She had picked at the appetizers, but then the encounter in the pool house had happened, then Reid and Nora's announcement and, well…here she was.

"More of your hidden kitchen talents?" she asked with a grin. "I am definitely on board with that."

"Then you're going to love these next few days. I plan on cooking for you every chance I get. I want a healthy baby, so I'm making sure his mama is cared for."

A healthy child. What she wouldn't give for that.

"You're going to spoil me and I won't want to leave."

Graham nipped once more at her lips. "That's the idea."

What? Did he mean...

Graham let go and went back to grab the bags. He headed up the stairs, leaving her staring after him as if he hadn't just dropped some veiled hint in her lap. Did he want to have her here longer than three days? Did he see their relationship as something more than physical? As something more than just sharing custody?

Hope blossomed inside her. Maybe this trip would be a turning point. Maybe letting him know exactly how she felt was just what they needed to move forward into a life together.

Graham froze at the edge of the couch where Eve lay on her side sleeping. He'd watched her from the kitchen as he cooked. She'd been sitting there reading a pregnancy magazine, then she'd stretched her feet out across the cushions. Now she was down for the count and the magazine had fallen to the floor.

Guilt slid through him. The ring he'd bought a week ago was in his room. He wanted to wait for the right moment to bring it out, to tell her he wanted their child to have his name.

They'd started out so hot for each other, and that hadn't changed. But the second Graham knew there was a child, he wasn't about to let anyone else get near what was his. This baby would have his name, no matter how he had to go about it.

But Eve's underlying defenselessness kept working its way further under his skin. When he wasn't with her, he was thinking about her—when he was with her, he didn't want to leave. He had never wanted a woman in his life permanently. Being married to his job was hard enough, but to try to sustain a relationship was damn near impossible.

For the first time in his life, Graham thought he actually wanted to try. Maybe he'd lost his mind. Perhaps he'd never had a chance where she was concerned. But no matter the reasoning or the path that led them here, Graham was tired of fighting this battle with himself.

Having Eve in his cabin, knowing she'd instantly loved this place the way he had only made him realize just how much they had in common.

He'd convinced her to come here immediately after the party. Maybe he should have waited until morning, but he was so afraid she'd start thinking and change her mind. So he'd whisked her off when she was exhausted. Sleep was exactly what she needed, and once she woke, they could start talking, planning.

Graham pulled the crocheted throw off the back of the sofa and placed it over Eve. Gerty had made this throw, and several other little items around the cabin. He'd wanted a piece of his past to be here. He'd wanted to hold on to the woman who had helped raise him and shape him into the man he was today.

Looking down on Eve's relaxed face, Graham couldn't help but wonder what Gerty would think of her. What would his mother think? No doubt both women would adore Eve. She was so easy to talk to. She may be president of one of the top real estate companies in Chicago, but it was her charm, her charisma and her determination that would keep her on top.

Sutton didn't deserve a daughter so perfect. He didn't deserve her loyalty. Sutton had used Graham's mother, not bothering to care what happened to her because he had his wife to go back to when he was done.

Graham hated Sutton more and more each time he thought of how easy it had been for the mogul to end things with Cynthia. She'd been pregnant, not that Sutton had stuck around to find out. She'd already had twins at home and was expecting another child. With the income from waitressing, there was no way she could have survived on her own...or been able to pay for an attorney if she were threatened with a custody battle. And she hadn't taken a dime from him for fear he'd sue for custody. She wouldn't have been able to battle Sutton in court.

Graham didn't blame his mother one bit for not telling the tycoon.

Gerty had seriously been the biggest blessing in all of their lives.

Eve reminded Graham so much of his grandma. Both women were strong. They both clung to their determination to get them through rough times. And they were both stubborn to a fault.

Graham took a seat in the leather chair, propped his feet on the ottoman and laced his hands over his abs. He was perfectly content to watch Eve rest. This is exactly what he wanted her to do.

Now he just had to figure out what he really wanted. Asking her to marry him may give her false hope. But on the other hand, he wasn't so sure his goals in marrying her were quite the same as they once were.

There was no denying that when she woke up, and once they started talking, the dynamics between them would change.

Graham just had to keep the upper hand and decide how much their lives were about to be altered.

Sixteen

Eve woke to blackness. There wasn't a single light on in the room. Where was she? She blinked a few times, sat up and quickly remembered. She'd fallen asleep on the couch in Graham's cabin.

The slightest glow from the porch lights filtered in through the windows. Eve sat up, turning her stiff neck from side to side. She didn't even recall lying down. She'd started reading a magazine, had gotten swept up by some article on how to make your own baby food, and that was the last thing she remembered.

Turning, Eve went still when she spotted Graham asleep in the chair across from her. His feet were propped on the oversize ottoman, his head tipped to one side. She wished there was more light so she could make out his facial features. Was he fully relaxed? When he'd fallen asleep in her bed, he always had those worry lines between his brows. Now that he was away, did he allow himself to completely let go?

Eve pulled at the throw caught around her legs. She hadn't put that there. An image of Graham covering her had a warmth spreading through her. The little ways he showed he cared couldn't be ignored. The way he cooked for her, opened up about his mother and Gerty, swept her away when life became too much...he was putting her needs first and she couldn't deny the tug on her heart.

Part of Eve wished they could just stay here forever. Ignore their families, ignore the entire mess with Sutton, Carson and the investigator Brooks had hired. Ignore the reality that her father was dying, that her sister was marrying the love of her life and everything was perfect for her. The entire family was thrilled for Nora, and Eve was, too. But there was still that fear that once everyone knew of Eve's pregnancy, she'd never be shown support. That she wouldn't experience such happiness. Her family wouldn't accept the fact that Graham was the father, and worse yet, that Eve had fallen for him.

Eve got to her feet, shaking out the throw. Moving around the ottoman, she started to lay the blanket over Graham. Instantly he gripped her wrist and pulled her down into his lap.

With a yelp, she fell right into the crook of his arm, her head to his shoulder.

"I thought you were asleep."

Graham adjusted her legs to settle them between his. "You thought wrong."

That low rumble vibrated from his chest. His fingertips trailed up her bare forearm. "How do you feel now?"

"Like I slept for days."

"Good. I want you to feel rejuvenated."

Eve relaxed fully against him. "I'm sorry I fell asleep when you were cooking. Did I ruin everything?"

"We can heat it back up whenever. It was late. You needed rest."

His fingertips continued to trail up and down her arm. When she shivered, Graham took the twisted blanket and gave it a flick to send it soaring out over their legs. He wrapped her tighter, in the blanket and his arms. Eve wasn't sure if this was some euphoric state from sleep or if this was really happening. Were they…snuggling? He wasn't trying to get her undressed, she wasn't straddling him and ripping his shirt off. They were just…doing nothing and it felt rather amazing.

"As much as I want you to relax and take it easy, I want to know something."

Eve stilled. "What?"

"About your first pregnancy."

Eve closed her eyes. She'd known the questions

would be coming, and he deserved to know. He'd given her time to prepare and hadn't immediately asked when Nora spilled the secret the other day.

Eve was ready to tell him now—*needed* to tell him. There was still a part of her that had to heal before she could move on. Not that she could fully recover from the loss of a child, but talking about the pain with the man she'd fallen in love with would go a long way to preparing her for the next chapter of her life.

"I was in love once," she started, then realized that wasn't the right thing to say. "Actually, I thought I was in love, but I had just been blindsided by lust and charm."

Graham remained silent, but kept his firm hold on her. She appreciated the darkened room, the fact she didn't have to look him in the eye when she was telling him about this portion of her life. There was a deeper intimacy about letting him in this way.

"I met Rick in college," she went on. "The attraction was instant. We dated for six months. I thought he was the one."

The words sounded so cold, so lifeless when she said them, but there was no other way to tell this story. That period of her life was gone and she was only left with the emotional scars.

"I found out I was pregnant." She'd never forget how happy she was to tell Rick. "I thought we'd marry, raise our family and live happily ever after." Eve pulled in a breath, toyed with the edging on the crocheted blanket. "When I told him I was pregnant, he was done with me. Apparently he was interested in being married to Sutton's daughter, but not so much in having a child. No, wait. He was more interested in being married to money. I was nothing."

"I want to kill him."

Eve smiled. "I appreciate the offer, but he married into money, then his wife cheated on him with the pool boy. Clichéd, but I did a small victory dance."

Graham chuckled, squeezing her tighter. "I had no idea you had such a ruthless side. Remind me never to cheat on you with the pool boy."

Smacking his arm, Eve continued. "Anyway, I was about six weeks pregnant then. I was scared, but my family was so supportive. I knew I'd be okay. Losing the baby never even entered my mind. Not once."

Graham slid his hand over hers, their fingers lacing over her stomach. That silent supportive gesture had tears burning her eyes.

"Nora, Grace and I had already picked out names," Eve whispered, her throat full of emotions. "I knew I wanted the nursery decorated in gray and yellow no matter what the sex of the baby was. When I was seventeen weeks, I went in for an ultrasound. The doctor's office had a new machine, one that had top-of-the-line imaging. I was so excited to see that little face, to find out what I was having."

When her voice broke, Eve bit her lip. She wanted

to hold it together. She wanted to show Graham that she was strong, but all those past emotions threatened to strangle her and end this conversation. Tremors racked her body as her eyes filled. There was no stopping the wave of memories and feelings as she relived the horrid day.

"Eve, don't—"

"No. I've come this far and you need to know." On a shaky breath, she continued, "The tech kept searching the screen and moving the device over my stomach almost frantically, and I knew something was wrong. Her face wasn't bright like when I'd first come in. At one point she excused herself and stepped out into the hall to ask someone to find the doctor. I knew. In my heart I knew something was wrong with my baby."

"What happened?"

"In simple terms, the cord came away from the amniotic sac. I don't know how far along I was when that happened. The doctor said my body still thought I was pregnant, so my uterus was still stretching." Eve sniffed, wiped at the tears on her cheeks. "I could've lost the baby a month earlier or I could've lost her that day. I honestly don't know. But I know I never want to live through that again. I can't."

"Oh, baby." Graham kissed the top of her head. "I don't even know what to say."

"Nothing can be said," she said. "People told me how sorry they were. They tried to say the right thing, but there isn't a right thing. I lost a piece of myself that day and the following days are a blur. I will never know that face. That's all I kept thinking. What did she look like?"

"She?"

Eve shrugged. "I don't know. I didn't ask. They had to perform a D&C the next day to remove all the tissue. I was getting prepped for surgery, wondering how things had gone from the highest mountain to the deepest pit I'd ever known, when the nurse had me sign a paper. It was a paper stating I gave them permission to dispose of any remains. *Dispose of.*"

"Eve, stop, please."

Tears slid down her face. "How could I sign a paper saying that was okay?" she asked, ignoring his plea. "This was my baby. I know I wasn't far enough along to have a funeral, but the wording was just so cold, so heartless. I'll never forget it."

Graham reached a hand up to wipe her wet cheeks, then smoothed her hair away from her face. "No more. Don't do this to yourself. I'm such a jerk for asking, but I thought I deserved to know. I should've thought of your feelings."

"No." Eve shifted in his arms to face him. "You did deserve to know. I wanted to tell you, but I didn't want to kill our mood here. I want you to know everything about me."

"I don't want you hurt," he murmured against her lips. "I can't stand it, Eve. Never again will you hurt like that."

Reaching up to cup his face, Eve tipped her head

back. "I hope I don't. I hope this baby is delivered full-term and healthy. I'm so afraid of how my family will react, how your brothers will take the news. I can handle quite a bit, but I won't let our child be in the cross fire."

Graham slid his thumb along her bottom lip. "Nobody will harm you or our child so long as I'm in the picture."

"And how long will that be?" she dared to ask.

In lieu of an answer, Graham kissed her gently. Eve instantly opened to him. He never had to ask, never had to persuade her. She was always ready for more contact, more of anything that had to do with Graham. He'd listened to her, he'd hurt for her and he was trying to make her forget if only for a short time.

When his hand trailed down to the hem of her shirt, she shifted. Without words, without the usual rush and frenzy, they were undressed and somehow ended up settled right back in the chair.

Eve rested a knee on either side of Graham's hips. "I love you."

She didn't mean to let loose with the words, but there was no holding them back.

"Eve—"

"No." She held a finger to his lips. "I don't need anything said in return. I've been completely open with you tonight and I wanted to get it all out. I needed to. Now show me how you were going to make me forget the rest of the world."

* * *

Graham couldn't get those words out of his mind. She loved him. Loved. Him.

No other woman, save for his mother and Gerty, had ever uttered those words to him before. He wasn't sure what to do, what to say. Had she not cut him off, what would've come out of his mouth in reply?

As he put breakfast together the following morning, Graham tried to pull himself together. This was what he'd been waiting for. She'd fallen in love with him and now all he had to do was make this relationship more official.

But after all she'd shared before her declaration of love, he didn't feel right about using her state of vulnerability to complete his plan. He needed to see what happened today, when they could talk more, explore the area together and just be themselves. Maybe...

What? Nothing had changed. He still wanted this child to have his name.

His cell vibrated on the counter. Brooks's name lit up the screen. Graham slid the casserole into the oven and answered his phone.

"Hello."

"Roman has a major lead. He thinks he has a name, but he's going to make a quick trip before he tells us to be sure."

Could this be it? After all this time could they have found their father?

Since Eve was still in bed where he'd left her, Graham put his phone on speaker so he could start cutting up the fruit.

"How soon will we know?" Graham asked, pulling out various bags of produce from the refrigerator.

"He's heading there today. Hopefully soon."

Graham slid a knife from the block on the counter. "I'm going to be nervous all day."

"Me, too," his brother said. "You ready to tell me where you are?"

"I'm at the cabin."

Brooks made a humming sound, one that mocked Graham and made him sorry he'd even admitted that much.

"With?" Brooks asked.

"None of your concern."

"It's my concern if you're sleeping with our enemy's daughter."

Graham glanced over his shoulder, thankful to see the living area still empty, which meant she was still in bed. "I'm with Eve, yes. But—"

"What the hell, man? What are you thinking?"

Graham didn't get a chance to reply before his brother went on. "Are you using her to try to get to Sutton?"

Graham slid the knife through the mango. "No. I wouldn't do that to her."

"Then what are you doing?"

Graham swallowed, deciding now was as good a time as any to come clean. "We're having a baby."

The explosion of cussing had Graham dropping the knife to the counter and taking the phone off speaker. "Calm the hell down," he barked.

"How long have you known and how could you keep something like this from me?" Brooks demanded.

"We kept our personal lives from everyone," Graham explained, leaning against the counter. "Between you, Carson and her family, we just wanted—"

"What? To mess around and not get caught?"

Basically.

"How'd that work out for you?"

Graham raked a hand through his bed head. "Listen, we're figuring things out and we needed to get away from the city."

"Sutton is not going to like this."

"No, he's not, but there's nothing that can change the fact." Graham stared at the stairs to the second floor, wondering how long she would sleep in. "I'm going to ask her to marry me."

"Are you a complete moron?" Brooks yelled. "Can you just slow down and think this through?"

"I have." Graham turned around and checked the casserole in the oven. "This baby is a Newport and will be raised as such. I'll do anything to make sure my child has my last name."

"So you love her?"

Graham shut the oven door again. "Love has nothing to do with it. The baby is what I'm concerned with."

When he turned back around, he froze. Eve stood on the other side of the kitchen island. All color had drained from her face as she clutched her silk robe together. The hurt in her eyes gutted him. He'd promised her no more pain, but he'd delivered a hell of a punch.

"I'll call you later," he told Brooks, ending the call without waiting for his brother's reply.

"Don't make excuses for what I wasn't supposed to hear," she told him, tipping her chin. "I'm flattered you want to marry me, but I think I'll decline. You see, I already made a fool of myself for one man I conceived a child with. I don't intend to do so again."

Graham started to step forward, but when she held up a hand and squared her shoulders, he stopped. The sheen in her eyes, the fact that she was fighting back tears, told him he'd completely ruined everything.

But he wasn't going down without a fight.

"Marriage isn't a terrible idea, Eve."

"For us? It's a terrible idea."

"Why?"

Crossing her arms over her chest, she pursed her lips as if choosing her next words carefully. Damn, she looked beautiful this morning. With her tousled hair, bright eyes, face devoid of any makeup, Eve was stunning. And she was pulling away. He couldn't let her end what he'd worked so hard to complete.

"I told you I loved you," she started, blinking away the tears. "I meant it. I didn't expect the words in return if you weren't feeling the same way. I understand. But to know you only want to marry me because of our baby, it's just so archaic. Did you think I'd keep your child from you?"

Graham didn't care what she wanted. He took a step toward her. "I didn't know what would happen, Eve. All I know is I'm going to be a father and I can't miss that. I can't."

Emotions he hadn't fully grasped came rushing at him. "I grew up without a father," he went on, still slowly closing the gap between them. "I've wondered for the past thirty-two years who my dad is, if he wanted me, if he even knows I exist. It's an empty void that I may never fill."

He stood so close now, Eve tipped her head back to look up into his eyes. The need for her understanding was so great, he had to find the right words. Any charm or wit he normally used to get his way wasn't possible here. All he could do was hope for the best when he opened up with complete and total honesty.

"Do you understand what I'm saying?" he asked.

"I can't let my child grow up without me. I don't want another man raising what's mine."

Eve's jaw clenched as she closed her eyes and pulled in a breath. "Do I look like I have men lined up outside my door?" she finally asked, glaring back at him. "Apparently you don't know me at all. And all I hear is how you want to give this child a name and treat him or her like your property. That's not how this works and that sure as hell isn't how a marriage should work."

"Eve—"

"No."

She backed away and held out both hands. Just as she did, she started to sway. Graham reached for her, but she pushed him away. She held her stomach with one hand and covered her mouth with the other. Alarmed, he waited to make sure she wasn't going to get sick or pass out. He was a complete ass for... well, everything. He remained close, though, in case she needed him. Not that she'd take his help now.

Moments later she pulled herself together and smoothed her hair from her face. "I'm going back to Chicago as soon as I call my pilot to come get me. Elite has a private helicopter at our disposal."

"I'll take you."

She was going. There was no stopping her. She'd erected walls he couldn't penetrate, not when she was so angry, so hurt. But he'd continue to chip away because he wasn't lying. There was no way he'd let his child grow up without a father.

"I'd rather call my pilot," she told him.

Eve turned on her heel and headed toward the stairs. Graham couldn't take his eyes off her. He silently pleaded for her to understand where he was coming from, why he was so adamant about marriage.

With her hand on the post, she turned to look over her shoulder. "You know what's sad? I thought you brought me here because you cared about me. I was naive enough to think you might have stronger feelings for me, that you wanted to get closer to me. Not because I was pregnant, but because of me."

Graham couldn't breathe, couldn't move.

Eve dropped her head between her shoulders, her grip tightening on the post. "You were using me all this time. I should've listened to my family when they first told me to stay away from you. But I defended you."

Now she turned to face him, her cheeks pink from tears, from anger. Graham hated himself at that moment. He hated the way he'd portrayed himself, the way he'd let her down when he'd promised that no one would hurt her again. He'd destroyed her. Destroyed the light in her eyes, the smile she so freely gave.

"I won't keep you from your child." Her voice shook, her chin quivered. "But I won't marry you, and from here on out, we're nothing to each other."

Without another word, she went up the stairs. Graham listened as the bedroom door clicked shut.

The gentle sound seemed to echo through the spacious house. It symbolized everything that had just happened. She'd put a barrier between them, and as he stood on the outside, he couldn't help but wonder how the hell he could ever fix this.

Seventeen

When he left her alone to pack, and then leave the cabin, Eve was even more hurt. She shouldn't have been surprised, but she was. He'd given up. Clearly he only wanted the child and she was an absolute fool to have believed otherwise.

But what hurt the most was that she still loved him. Well, she loved the man she thought he was. He'd been so caring, so amazing these past couple of weeks, but one overheard phone call had revealed the truth.

Eve had been home only a day, but she'd called her sisters and her father for a family meeting. Dr. Wilde had told Eve that Sutton was resting, but he was having a good day and to come on by. Grace and Nora were meeting Eve at the Winchester estate.

As Eve stood outside the front door, she fought back her nerves. Had it only been two nights since she was here for a party? A party announcing her sister's engagement. A party Graham had crashed, and then he'd taken her...

No. There would be no more thinking along those lines. Whatever they'd shared in the past was best left there. Their affair had started out so fast, so intense, there was no way it could've lasted or even morphed into something with deeper meaning. Eve cursed herself for getting so caught up in romanticizing the secret of it all.

Gathering up her courage, she let herself in and headed straight to her father's study. Grace and Nora were already there. Grace adjusted the throw on her father's legs and Nora glanced up, catching Eve's eye. A soft smile from her sister was all Eve needed to get through this. Having Nora here was a huge help since she already knew.

Grace glanced up when Eve shut the door. "Is everything okay?" she asked. "You sounded strange on the phone."

Eve met her father's questioning eyes. "I'm fine, but I have something I need to tell you all."

Grace straightened, taking hold of their father's hand. "You're scaring me. Are you sick, too?"

"What? No." She hadn't meant to scare them. "I'm pregnant."

Silence. Not a word was said as her sisters and father just stared back at her.

"I'm at seven weeks," she went on, in a rush to fill the dead air. "The doctor has assured me that everything looks great, but I'm scared." There, she'd said it. "I need your help and support, no judgment, please. I can't deal with it right now."

"Because Graham is the father?" Grace asked.

Eve bit her lip in an attempt to battle back the emotions. Afraid to speak, she merely nodded.

"He didn't say a word when he was here the other day," her father chimed in. "Does he know?"

Eve moved farther into the room. "What? He was here?"

"With Brooks and Carson."

Eve's mind spun. He'd been to see her father and hadn't said a word. The betrayals kept on coming. He'd been sleeping with her, telling her everything she wanted to know, but sneaking to see her father behind her back.

"Was he pressuring you?" Eve demanded as she eased a hip onto the side of the bed.

"I actually invited Carson here," he stated. "I wanted a chance to tell him I'm sorry, to see if there was a possibility of connecting now that I know for sure he's my son. I didn't want to die without him knowing that I loved his mother, that I would've fought had I known he existed."

Eve listened as her father exposed his emotions. She'd never heard him this passionate about anything other than business. Sutton Winchester was one of the most prominent, powerful men in Chicago and he'd been deprived of raising his own child.

Was that truly what Graham had thought she'd do? Had she ever indicated she'd be so heartless? He'd been determined to marry her, so much so he'd swept her away on a trip away from everything she knew. She'd been easily swayed because she honestly thought he cared about her, when in reality he was softening her, getting her to fall for him, all so he could convince her to marry him.

"Wait, has he pushed you away?" Grace asked.

"No." Eve took her father's other hand. "He... it's complicated. I don't want to go into the details, but—"

"Complicated? You two were on the same page when I saw you the other morning."

Eve glanced at Nora, who had pulled up a chair by their father's bed. Grace and Sutton both turned to Nora.

"She knew?" Grace asked.

Nora shrugged, sending Eve an apologetic glance. "I happened to stop by her house when Graham was there making breakfast for her."

"Things have changed since then," Eve explained. "All I need right now is for you guys to know I won't let Elite down. I'm 100 percent committed to the company and—"

"This baby comes before any company."

Eve stilled at her father's words. He'd never said

anything like that. He was loyal to his family, yes, but he always put business first. Always.

"I can handle both," she assured him.

"I'm sure you can." He turned his hand over and held on to hers. "But I want a healthy grandbaby. I want you to take care of yourself. We have enough staff that can assist you, so put some of the burden on them. That's my greatest regret—not having been there more for my kids."

Eve glanced to her sisters, who had both started tearing up.

"When you're faced with the end, you start thinking about the beginning," he went on. "And if I could go back, I'd definitely put some work off onto my assistants so I could be with you all more. Learn from my mistakes, Eve. Take care of yourself."

"That's what I've been telling her."

Eve jerked at the familiar voice behind her. Graham stood in the doorway with the butler right behind him.

"I tried to stop him, Mr. Winchester," the poor man explained.

"It's fine," Sutton replied. "Close the door and leave us."

Eve continued to stare at Graham, who hadn't taken his eyes off her. "What are you doing here?" she demanded, coming to her feet. "You can't just barge in here—"

"I can. And I did."

Eve didn't risk looking behind her to her sisters

or father. The tension in the room had multiplied, threatening to take over.

"I don't want you here," she told him, pulling her cardigan tighter around her. As if such a simple gesture could keep any more pain from seeping in.

"I realize that." His tone softened as he inched closer. "I know I hurt you, but the moment you left I knew I wasn't finished."

Eve didn't have much energy for a battle. The past forty-eight hours had been hellacious at best.

"Then say what you want to say and get out."

He'd reached her now, but didn't touch her. "I meant I wasn't finished with us."

Eve stared into those striking eyes that had first drawn her in. "There is no us. If that's all, then leave."

"Do you two want to go outside for privacy?" Grace asked from behind Eve.

"No," both Eve and Graham said at the same time.

"I don't care who hears me," he went on, keeping his eyes locked on hers. "When you left yesterday I knew I had to take drastic measures to get you back. So, if I have to make a fool of myself in front of your family, then so be it."

Eve didn't want to hear it, though she wouldn't mind him looking like a fool considering she'd been played for one.

"I'm not discussing the baby's last name. I know that's all you care about." Eve stepped back because being this close, knowing she still loved him but couldn't touch him was agonizing. "If you'll excuse me, I'm visiting my father."

Eve had just turned away when Graham's soft, "I love you," hit her hard.

Frozen in her steps, she looked to her sisters, her father, to see if she'd heard correctly. And saw three pairs of eyes wide with shock staring back at her. Yeah, he'd said that.

Eve looked back over her shoulder, her heart aching more than she'd ever known possible. "That was cruel," she whispered as tears clogged her throat. "Throwing those words around won't make me marry you."

Graham reached for her, turning her to face him fully. "I'm not proposing. I love you, Eve. I want to be with you. Not for the baby, for you."

If he'd said those words two days ago she'd have believed him. "Revelation has certainly come at a convenient time."

His hands curled around her shoulders as he stepped in closer. Her entire body brushed against his, as if she needed the physical reminder of how much she'd missed his touch.

"Nothing about us has been convenient," he told her. "I didn't want a child, a relationship, but now I can't live without either. I don't want to try. I know I hurt you, I know I destroyed everything we'd started building, but I'm asking for another chance."

Eve couldn't say anything. What was there to say at this point? He was a shark in the courtroom because he knew the exact thing to say at precisely the right time.

If she even thought he was serious, she'd wrap her arms around him and start fresh. But she knew better. Graham was only looking out for his best interests where the baby was concerned.

"You need to go," she whispered.

The muscle in his jaw clenched as he nodded, dropping his hands from her shoulders. "I'm not giving up, Eve. I love you. I've only had two women in my life who heard those words from me."

His mother and Gerty.

Eve turned away from him and went back to her father's bedside. She listened to Graham's footsteps as he left the room. Once the door was closed behind him, Eve couldn't stop the emotions from washing over her.

"I hate him," she sniffed. "I'm sorry you had to see that."

Her father reached for her, tipping her chin up so she could look him in the eyes. "I'm not sorry at all. I saw a man who loves a woman. I saw a man who stood in the same room as his sworn enemy and didn't give a damn what anyone else thought."

"He's only saying those things because he wants to marry me so the baby will have his name."

"The baby can have his name without marriage," Grace pointed out. "He could fight you for custody in court and probably win, if that's the way he wanted to go about it."

Eve knew all of this. She wasn't stupid, wasn't ignorant when it came to laws. But she had been blindsided and refused to let Graham have another swipe at her.

"I'll agree he didn't go about things the right way," her father said, swiping a tear from her face. "But men are fools when they're in love. Most of the time they don't even know it until they've lost someone."

Eve knew her father was referring to Cynthia. There were no secrets about the fact that Eve's parents didn't love each other. Eve fully believed that her father was in love with Graham's mother at one time. But he'd let her go.

"I can't let him back in," she whispered.

"You can't let him out," Nora countered. "He loves you, Eve."

Eve met the eyes of her family. "Are you all defending him?"

Sutton smiled. "I'm just as shocked as you are, but I want my daughter and grandchild to be happy. When I saw the way he looked at you, the way he didn't care how he laid his feelings on the line, I knew he loved you. Any man who is that strong and passionate is exactly what I want for you."

Eve couldn't believe what she was hearing. "You want me to forgive him? Just like that? It's that easy?"

When her fathered smiled, wrinkles formed around his sad eyes. "I want you to follow your heart. I don't believe Graham will give up and that has everything to do with his feelings for you. Grace was right. He could fight you in court, where things would get ugly if he only wanted the child to have his name. I don't think he realized how much he cared for you until you left."

Eve shook her head. "I can't just take him back. Right now, I only want to be here with you guys. I want to visit and laugh and… I don't know. Pick out nursery themes."

"I'm thrilled that's your attitude," Nora said, reaching over to squeeze Eve's shoulder. "This baby will be perfectly healthy and come home to a beautiful room and a family who loves her."

"Her?" their father asked, raising his brows.

"I think Eve is having a girl, too," Grace laughed. "Another Winchester girl? That has a nice ring to it."

Eve didn't care about the sex, she just wanted a healthy baby. Now more than ever, she wanted that happiness in her life. She prayed her father would live long enough to see her child, but the odds were against them.

For now, though, she wouldn't dwell on the sorrow. She'd live in the moment.

Later she'd deal with the ache…and she'd deal with Graham.

Three days had passed since she'd seen Graham… since he'd exposed himself before her family. But he'd texted her. He'd checked on her, asked if she was eating, joked that he'd send over some of the fried apples she loved. He didn't tell her he loved her again, didn't pressure her to meet him or to make a decision regarding this relationship they'd thrown up in the air and left hanging.

He'd genuinely been…well, caring. And she was positive this wasn't some game to him. He wasn't using her. Eve realized that if he'd wanted to use her all along, then he would've tried to use her to get closer to her father. If he was that sure her father held secrets about Graham's past, then he could have easily used his charms and sneaky maneuvers to find out what she knew. Or have her find out what her father knew.

He'd done neither. When they were together, he'd avoided the topic. It had taken Eve two restless, sleepless nights to replay their last seven weeks. There were no red flags, nothing other than an intense affair and unexpected emotions.

Now she stood in the lobby of his building, clutching a photo, more scared than she'd ever been in her life. This was the biggest risk she'd ever taken, but this could also be the greatest thing to ever happen to her.

By the time Eve reached the top floor and stood outside the only door in the hall, she was a little more under control…until the door swung open and Graham stood there in a pair of running shorts, beads of sweat running down his chest.

"Doorman told me you were on your way up," he explained. "I was on the treadmill."

Eve still didn't say anything. Now that she was here, all the speeches she'd rehearsed vanished from her mind. The picture in her hand crinkled, drawing her attention to the reason she needed to gather up that Winchester courage.

"I, um…can I come in?"

Graham stepped back, opening the door wider. The second she passed by him, she was assaulted with that sexy, sweaty, masculine scent. She wanted this to be easy, didn't want a messy reunion…if he'd take her. They'd been through so much already, Eve wasn't even sure a relationship was possible.

Eve crossed the spacious entryway and stepped down into the living area. Her eyes were fixed on the skyline.

"I never got to appreciate the view in Tennessee," she muttered. "I was numb when I left."

When he said nothing, Eve turned, only to find he'd moved in closer behind her.

"I was still numb when I saw you at my dad's house," she went on. "But then I realized you didn't have to be there. You could've let me go, could've waited and fought me."

His intense stare hit her as fiercely as his words. "I'd never fight you, Eve."

"I'm tired," she whispered. "Tired of worrying, tired of questioning and tired of wondering what we're doing."

Graham reached for her, pulling her into his arms. She didn't care that his chest was damp with sweat. All she cared about was that he didn't seem to have changed his mind.

"Put it all on me," he murmured against her ear. "Every fear, every worry, give it to me. I want to be everything for you, Eve."

She eased back, hope spreading through her. "Can our lives be that easy? Can we make this work?"

"I'll do anything to have you in my life, Eve. Anything. Not just the baby, but you." He framed her face with his strong hands. "I've never loved a woman the way I love you. I've never wanted to. But we fit, Eve. We get each other and I can't imagine life without you."

Sliding the black-and-white image between them, she held up the picture for him to see. "This is for you."

Graham took a step back and stared at it. It was a sonogram of their baby. His eyes instantly misted as he slowly reached for the glossy image.

"I didn't think you'd had the appointment yet."

"I called the doctor for a favor." Eve smiled, unable to stop herself as she saw how in love Graham was with this child already. "I wanted to give you this. I wanted you to know that we are both yours if you'll have us. If you can forgive me for doubting you, for doubting us."

His eyes instantly sought hers. "There's nothing to forgive. I'm the one who nearly ruined the greatest thing that's ever happened to me. I won't ask you to marry me. But know that the second you want to, I'm ready."

Eve started to say something, but he held up his hand. "Because I love you both. I want to build a life with you, raise all the babies you want."

"My father defended you," she told him.

Graham looked shocked. "He did?"

"I know you think he has a secret about your father, but this disease, it's changed him. I—I'll go with you if you want to ask him. He won't lie to me."

Graham pulled her in once more. "I have everything I need right here. I won't put you between your father and me. Besides, Brooks has a lead with the investigator."

Eve pulled back. "That's great."

Graham smiled. "Roman is out now searching and he's pretty sure he has the name we've been searching for."

"Oh, Graham. Are you excited?"

"I am." He kissed the top of her head. "But not nearly as excited as I was the second I knew you were here to see me. Don't leave. Stay with me."

Eve leaned up on her tiptoes to kiss him. "Maybe we should start with a shower and then talk."

Graham set the picture down on the accent table and scooped her up into his arms. "That's the best idea I've ever heard."

* * * * *

Don't miss a single installment of the
DYNASTIES: THE NEWPORTS *series.*
Passion and chaos consume a
Chicago real estate empire.

SAYING YES TO THE BOSS
by Andrea Laurence

AN HEIR FOR THE BILLIONAIRE
by Kat Cantrell

CLAIMED BY THE COWBOY
by Sarah M. Anderson

HIS SECRET BABY BOMBSHELL
by Jules Bennett

BACK IN THE ENEMY'S BED
by Michelle Celmer

THE TEXAN'S ONE NIGHT STAND-OFF
by Charlene Sands

Available now from Harlequin Desire!

If you're on Twitter, tell us what you think
of Harlequin Desire! #harlequindesire

COMING NEXT MONTH FROM

Available November 8, 2016

#2479 HOLD ME, COWBOY

Copper Ridge • by Maisey Yates

Rich-as-sin cowboy Sam McCormack wants nothing to do with ice princess Madison West, but when they're snowed in together at a mountain retreat, their red-hot attraction quickly burns through all their misconceptions...

#2480 ONE HEIR...OR TWO?

Billionaires and Babies • by Yvonne Lindsay

As promised, Kayla became the surrogate mother for her late sister's baby—and she's expecting again! But when complications arise, the only person who can help is the sexy billionaire donor who doesn't yet know he's a dad...

#2481 HIS SECRETARY'S LITTLE SECRET

The Lourdes Brothers of Key Largo • by Catherine Mann

Organizing Easton Lourdes's workaholic life is a full-time job, and secretary Portia Soto is the best at keeping things professional. But when a hurricane sends her into her boss's arms—and his bed—the consequences will change everything...

#2482 HOLIDAY BABY SCANDAL

Mafia Moguls • by Jules Bennett

Dangerous Ryker Barrett owes the O'Shea family everything—and he proves his loyalty by keeping his hands off Laney O'Shea. Until he not only seduces her, but gets her pregnant, too! Will his dark past keep him from forever with her?

#2483 HIS PREGNANT CHRISTMAS BRIDE

The Billionaires of Black Castle • by Olivia Gates

Ivan left the woman he loved once, to protect them both. But when he saves her from an attack, he can no longer stay away. Will keeping Anastasia as his bride mean overcoming the sinister events that shaped him?

#2484 BACK IN THE ENEMY'S BED

Dynasties: The Newports • by Michelle Celmer

Roman betrayed Grace years ago. So when the wealthy ex-soldier swaggers back into her life, she's prepared to turn the tables on him. But she can't resist the unexpected desire between them—even as his secrets threaten to tear them apart...

REQUEST YOUR FREE BOOKS!
2 FREE NOVELS PLUS 2 FREE GIFTS!

HARLEQUIN®

Desire

ALWAYS POWERFUL, PASSIONATE AND PROVOCATIVE

YES! Please send me 2 FREE Harlequin® Desire novels and my 2 FREE gifts (gifts are worth about $10). After receiving them, if I don't wish to receive any more books, I can return the shipping statement marked "cancel." If I don't cancel, I will receive 6 brand-new novels every month and be billed just $4.55 per book in the U.S. or $5.24 per book in Canada. That's a savings of at least 13% off the cover price! It's quite a bargain! Shipping and handling is just 50¢ per book in the U.S. and 75¢ per book in Canada.* I understand that accepting the 2 free books and gifts places me under no obligation to buy anything. I can always return a shipment and cancel at any time. Even if I never buy another book, the two free books and gifts are mine to keep forever.

225/326 HDN GH2P

Name	(PLEASE PRINT)
Address	Apt. #
City	State/Prov.	Zip/Postal Code

Signature (if under 18, a parent or guardian must sign)

Mail to the **Reader Service:**

IN U.S.A.: P.O. Box 1867, Buffalo, NY 14240-1867
IN CANADA: P.O. Box 609, Fort Erie, Ontario L2A 5X3

Want to try two free books from another line?
Call 1-800-873-8635 or visit www.ReaderService.com.

* Terms and prices subject to change without notice. Prices do not include applicable taxes. Sales tax applicable in N.Y. Canadian residents will be charged applicable taxes. Offer not valid in Quebec. This offer is limited to one order per household. Not valid for current subscribers to Harlequin Desire books. All orders subject to credit approval. Credit or debit balances in a customer's account(s) may be offset by any other outstanding balance owed by or to the customer. Please allow 4 to 6 weeks for delivery. Offer available while quantities last.

Your Privacy—The Reader Service is committed to protecting your privacy. Our Privacy Policy is available online at www.ReaderService.com or upon request from the Reader Service.

We make a portion of our mailing list available to reputable third parties that offer products we believe may interest you. If you prefer that we not exchange your name with third parties, or if you wish to clarify or modify your communication preferences, please visit us at www.ReaderService.com/consumerchoice or write to us at Reader Service Preference Service, P.O. Box 9062, Buffalo, NY 14240-9062. Include your complete name and address.

HDI5

"Are you going to suggest that I need *you*?" she asked,
her voice choked.

Lightning streaked through his blood, and in that
moment, he was lost. It didn't matter that he thought
she was insufferable, a prissy little princess who didn't
appreciate anything she had. It didn't matter that he was
up here to work.

All that mattered was he hadn't touched a woman in a
long time, and Madison West was so close all he would
have to do was shift his weight slightly and he'd be able
to take her into his arms.

"Well," he said, "you have a couple of the essential
ingredients to have yourself a pretty fun evening. All you
seem to be missing is a good man. I'm not very nice,
Madison," he said, leaning in, "but I could damn sure
show you a good time."

She should throw him out. She looked over at him, and her libido made a dash to the foreground. That was the problem. He irritated her. He was exactly the kind of man she didn't like. He was cocky; he was rough and crude. However, there was something about the way he looked in a tight T-shirt that made a mockery of all that very certain hatred.

"Are you going to take off your coat and stay awhile?" That question, asked in a faintly mocking tone, sent a dart of tension straight down between her thighs.

She could *not* take off her coat. Because she was wearing nothing more than a little scrap of red lace underneath it. And now it was all she could think of. "It's cold," she snapped. "Maybe if you went to work getting the electricity back on rather than standing here making terrible double entendres I would be able to take off my coat."

The maddening man raised his eyebrows, shooting her a look that clearly said Suit yourself, then set about looking for the fuse box. She let out an exasperated sigh and followed his path, stopping when she saw him leaning against the wall, a little metal door between the logs open as he examined the switches inside.

"It's not a fuse. That means there's something else going on." He slammed the door shut and turned back to look at her. "You should come over to my cabin."

Don't miss
HOLD ME, COWBOY
by New York Times *bestselling author Maisey Yates,*
available November 2016 wherever
Harlequin® Desire books and ebooks are sold.

www.Harlequin.com

Whatever You're Into… Passionate Reads

Looking for more passionate reads from Harlequin®?
Fear not! Harlequin® Presents, Harlequin® Desire and
Harlequin® Blaze offer you irresistible romance stories
featuring powerful heroes.

❤HARLEQUIN *Presents*®

Do you want alpha males, decadent glamour and jet-set
lifestyles? Step into the sensational, sophisticated world of
Harlequin® Presents, where sinfully tempting heroes ignite a
fierce and wickedly irresistible passion!

❤HARLEQUIN *Desire*

Harlequin® Desire novels are powerful, passionate and
provocative contemporary romances set against a backdrop of
wealth, privilege and sweeping family saga. Alpha heroes with
a soft side meet strong-willed but vulnerable heroines amid a
dramatic world of divided loyalties, high-stakes conflict and
intense emotion.

❤HARLEQUIN *Blaze*

Harlequin® Blaze stories sizzle with strong heroines and
irresistible heroes playing the game of modern love and lust.
They're fun, sexy and always steamy.

Be sure to check out our full selection of books
within each series every month!

www.Harlequin.com

HPASSION2016